Robert Dodsley, William Shenstone

The Works in Verse and Prose of William Shenstone, Esq.

in two volumes

Robert Dodsley, William Shenstone

The Works in Verse and Prose of William Shenstone, Esq.
in two volumes

ISBN/EAN: 9783337369699

Printed in Europe, USA, Canada, Australia, Japan

Cover: Foto ©Andreas Hilbeck / pixelio.de

More available books at **www.hansebooks.com**

THE

W O R K S

IN

VERSE AND PROSE

OF

WILLIAM SHENSTONE, Esq;

Moſt of which were never before printed.

IN TWO VOLUMES.

VOLUME II.

—————— *His ego longos*
Cantando puerum memini me condere ſoles. VIRG.

EDINBURGH:

Printed for ALEXANDER DONALDSON.

MDCCLXV.

CONTENTS.

Of

CONTENTS.

VERSES TO MR SHENSTONE.

E S S A Y S

O N

M E N, M A N N E R S,

A N D

T H I N G S.

✢ ✢✢ ✢✢✢✢✢✢✢ ✢✢✢ ✢✢✢✢✢ ✢✢✢ ✢✢✢

On Publications.

IT is not unamufing to confider the feveral a-
pologies that people make when they commence authors. It is taken for granted
that on every publication there is at leaft a feeming violation of modefty; a prefumption, on the
writer's fide, that he is able to inftruct or to entertain the world; which implies a fuppofition
that he can communicate, what they cannot
draw from their own reflections.

To remove any prejudice this might occafion,
has been the general intent of prefaces. Some
we find extremely folicitous to claim acquaintance with their reader; addreffing him by the
moft tender and endearing appellations. He is
in general ftyled the moft loving, candid, and
courteous creature that ever breathed; with a
view, doubtlefs, that he will deferve the compli-

ment ; and that his favour may be fecured at the expenfe of his better judgment.   Mean and idle expectation ! The accidental elopements and adventures of a compofition ; the danger of an imperfect and furreptitious publication ; the pref- fing and indifcreet inftances of friends ; the pious and well-meant frauds of acquaintance ; with the irrefiftible commands of perfons in high life ; have been excufes often fubftituted in place of the real motives, vanity and hunger.

THE moft allowable reafons for appearing thus in public, are either the advantage or a- mufement of our fellow-creatures ; or our own private emolument and reputation.

A MAN poffeffed of intellectual talents would be more blameable in confining them to his own private ufe, than the mean-fpirited mifer, that did the fame by his money. The latter is indeed obliged to bid adieu to what he communicates ; the former enjoys his treafures, even while he renders others the better for them. A compofi- tion that enters the world with a view of impro- ving or amufing it, (I mean only, amufing it in a polite or innocent way), has a claim to our ut- moft indulgence, even though it fail of the effect intended.

WHEN a writer's private intereft appears the motive of his publication, the reader has a larger fcope for accufation, if he be a fufferer. Who- ever pays for thoughts, which this kind of wri- ters may be faid to vend, has room enough to complain, if he be difappointed of his bargain. He has no revenge, but ridicule ; and, contrary to the practice in other cases, to make the worst of a bad bargain.

WHEN the love of fame acts upon a man of genius, the case appears to stand thus. The generality of the world, distinguished by the name of readers, observe with a reluctance not unnatural, a person raising himself above them. All men have some desire of fame, and fame is grounded on comparison: Every one then is somewhat inclined to dispute his title to a superiority; and to disallow his pretensions upon the discovery of a flaw. Indeed, a fine writer, like a luminous body, may be beneficial to the person he enlightens; but, it is plain, he renders the opacity of the other more discernible.—Examination, however, is a sort of turnpike in the way to fame, where, though a writer be a while detained, and part with a trifle from his pocket, he finds in return a more commodious and easy road to the temple.

WHEN, therefore, a man is conscious of ability to serve his country, or believes himself possessed of it, (for there is no previous test on this occasion), he has no room to hesitate, or need to make apology.—When self-interest inclines a man to print, he should consider that the purchaser expects a pennyworth for his penny; and has reason to asperse his honesty if he finds himself deceived.—Also, that it is possible to publish a book of no value, which is too frequently the product of such mercenary people.—When fame is the principal object of our devotion, it should be considered whether our character is like to

gain

gain in point of wit, what it will probably lofe in point of modefty : otherwife we fhall be cenfu- red of vanity more than famed for genius ; and deprefs our character while we ftrive to raife it.

AFTER all, there is a propenfity in fome to communicate their thoughts without any view at all : the more fanguine of thefe employ the prefs ; the lefs lively are contented with being impertinent in converfation.

On

On the Teſt of popular opinion.

I HAPPEN to fall into company with a citizen, a courtier, and an academic.

SAYS the citizen, I am told continually of taſte, refinement, and politeneſs; but methinks the vulgar and illiterate generally approve the ſame productions with the connoiſſeurs. One rarely finds a landſcape, a building, or a play that has charms for the critic excluſive of the mechanic. But on the other hand one readily remarks ſtudents who labour to be dull, depraving their native reliſh by the very means they uſe to refine it. The vulgar may not indeed be capable of giving the reaſons why a compoſition pleaſes them. That mechanical diſtinction they leave to the connoiſſeur. But they are at all times, methinks, judges of the beauty of an effect, a part of knowledge in moſt reſpects allowedly more genteel than that of the operator.

SAYS the courtier, I cannot anſwer for every individual inſtance; but I think, moderately ſpeaking, the vulgar are generally in the wrong. If they happen to be otherwiſe, it is principally owing to their implicit reliance on the ſkill of their ſuperiours: and this has ſometimes been ſtrangely effectual in making them imagine they reliſh perfection. In ſhort, if ever they judge well, it is at the time they leaſt preſume to frame opinions for themſelves.

IT is true they will pretend to taſte an object

which.

which they know their betters do. But then they confider fome perfons judgment as a certain ftandard or rule; they find the object exactly tally; and this demonftrated appearance of beauty affords them fome fmall degree of fatisfaction.

It is the fame with regard to the appetite from which the metaphor of tafte is borrowed. " Such a foup or ollio," fay they, " is much in " vogue, and if you do not like it, you muft " learn to like it."

But in poetry, for inftance, it is urged, that the vulgar difcover the fame beauties with the man of reading.

Now, half or more of the beauties of poetry depend on metaphor or allufion, neither of which, by a mind uncultivated, can be applied to their proper counterparts. Their beauty, of confequence, is like a picture to a blind man.

How many of thefe peculiarities in poetry turn upon a knowledge of philofophy and hiftory: and let me add thefe latent beauties give the moft delight to fuch as can unfold them.

I might launch out much further in regard to the narrow limits of their apprehenfions. — What I have faid may exclude their infallibility; and it is my opinion they are feldom right.

The academic fpoke little, but to the purpofe; afferting that all ranks and ftations have their different fpheres of judging: That a clown of native tafte enough to relifh Handel's Meffiah, might unqueftionably be fo inftructed as to relifh it yet more: That an author, before he prints,
fhould

ſhould not flatter himſelf with a confuſed expectation of pleaſing both the vulgar and the polite;
few things, in compariſon, being capable of doing both in any great degree : That he ſhould
always meaſure out his plan for the ſize of un-
derſtanding he would fit. If he can content himſelf with the mob, he is pretty ſure of numbers
for a time. If he write with more abundant e-
legance, it may eſcape the organs of ſuch readers ; but he will have a chance for ſuch applauſe
as will more ſenſibly affeƈt him. Let a writer
then in his firſt performances negleƈt the idea of
profit, and the vulgar's applauſe entirely : Let
him addreſs him to the judicious few, and then
profit and the mob will follow. His firſt appearance on the ſtage of letters will ingroſs the poli-
ter compliments ; and his latter will partake of
the irrational huzza.

On allowing MERIT in OTHERS.

A CERTAIN gentleman was expressing himself as follows.

I CONFESS I have no great taste for poetry; but if I had, I am apt to believe I should read no other poetry than that of Mr Pope. The rest but barely arrive at a mediocrity in their art; and to be sure poetry of that stamp, can afford but slender pleasure.

I KNOW not, says another, what may be the gentleman's motive to give this opinion: but I am persuaded numbers pretend the same through mere jealousy or envy.

A READER considers an author, as one who lays claim to a superiour genius. He is ever inclined to dispute it, because if he happen to invalidate his title, he has at least one superiour the less. Now, though a man's absolute merit may not depend upon the inferiority of another, yet his comparative worth varies in regard to that of other people. Self-love, therefore, is ever attentive to pursue the single point of admitting no more into the class of superiours, than it is impossible to exclude. Could it even limit the number to one, they would soon attempt to undermine him. Even Mr Pope had been refused his honours, but that the very constraint, and even absurdity of people's shutting their eyes, grew as disagreeable to them, as that excellence, which, when open, they could not but discover.

BUT.

But self-love obtains its wishes in another respect also. It hereby not only depresses the characters of many that have wrote, but stifles the genius of such as might hereafter rise from amongst our inferiours.

Let us not deny to Mr Pope the praises which a person enamoured of poetry would bestow on one that excelled in it : But let us consider Parnaffus rather as a republic than a monarchy ; where, although some may be in possession of a more cultivated spot, yet where others may possess land as fruitful, upon equal cultivation.

On the whole, let us reflect, that the nature of the soil, and the extent of its fertility, must remain undiscovered, if the gentleman's desponding principle should meet with approbation.

Mr Pope's chief excellence lies in what I would term consolidating or condensing sentences, yet preserving ease and perspicuity. In smoothness of verse, perhaps, he has been equalled ; in regard to invention, excelled.

Add to this, if the writers of antiquity may be esteemed our truest models, Mr Pope is much more witty, and less simple, than his own Horace appears in any of his writings ; more witty, and less simple, than the modern Monf. Boileau, who claimed the merit of uniting the style of Juvenal and Persius with that of Horace.

Satire gratifies self-love. This was one source of his popularity ; and he seems even so very conscious of it as to stigmatize many inoffensive characters.

The circumstance of what is called alliteration,

tion, and the nice adjuftment of the paufe, have confpired to charm the prefent age, but have at the fame time given his verfes a very cloying peculiarity.

But, perhaps, we muft not expect to trace the flow of Waller, the landfcape of Thomfon, the fire of Dryden, the imagery of Shakefpear, the fimplicity of Spenfer, the courtlinefs of Prior, the humour of Swift, the wit of Cowley, the delicacy of Addifon, the tendernefs of Otway, and the invention, the fpirit, and fublimity of Milton, joined in any fingle writer. The lovers of poetry, therefore, fhould allow fome praife to thofe who fhine in any branch of it, and only range them into claffes according to that fpecies in which they fhine.

Quare agite, O juvenes !

Banifh the felf-debafing principle, and fcorn the difingenuity of readers. Humility has depreffed many a genius into an hermit ; but never yet raifed one into a poet of eminence.

T H E

THE IMPROMPTU.

THE critics, however unable to fix the time which it is moſt proper to allow for the action of an epic poem, have univerſally agreed that ſome certain ſpace is not to be exceeded. Concerning this, Ariſtotle, their great Lycurgus, is entirely ſilent. Succeeding critics have done little more than cavil concerning the time really taken up by the greateſt epic writers ; that, if they could not frame a law, they might at leaſt eſtabliſh a precedent of unexceptionable authority. Homer, ſay they, confined the action of his Iliad, or rather his action may be reduced to the ſpace of two months. His Odyſſey, according to Boſſu and Dacier, is extended to eight years. Virgil's Æneid has raiſed very different opinions in his commentators. Taſſo's poem includes a ſummer.—— But leaving ſuch knotty points to perſons that appear born for the diſcuſſion of them, let us endeavour to eſtabliſh laws that are more likely to be obeyed, than controverted. An epic writer, though limited in regard to the time of his action, is under no ſort of reſtraint with regard to the time he takes to finiſh his poem. Far different is the caſe with a writer of Impromptu's. He indeed is allowed all the liberties that he can poſſibly take in his compoſition, but is rigidly circumſcribed with regard to the ſpace in which it is completed. And no wonder ; for whatever degree of poignancy may be required in this compoſition, its peculiar merit

rit

rit muft ever be relative to the expedition with which it is produced.

It appears indeed to me to have the nature of that kind of fallad, which certain eminent adepts in chymiftry have contrived to raife, while a joint of mutton is roafting. We do not allow our-felves to blame its unufual flatnefs and infipidity, but extol the little flavour it has, confidering the time of its vegetation.

An extemporaneous poet, therefore, is to be judged, as we judge a race-horfe ; not by the gracefulnefs of his motion, but the time he takes to finifh his courfe. The beft critic upon earth may err in determining his precife degree of me-rit, if he have neither a ftop-watch in his hand, nor a clock within his hearing.

To be a little more ferious : An extemporane-ous piece ought to be examined by a compound ratio, or a medium compounded of its real worth, and the fhortnefs of the time that is employed in its production. By this rule even Virgil's poem may be in fome fort deemed extemporaneous, as the time he took to perfect fo extraordinary a compofition, confidered with its real worth, ap-pears fhorter than the time employed to write the diftichs of Cofconius.

On the other hand, I cannot allow this title to the flafhes of my friend S —— in 'the magazine, which have no fort of claim to be called verfes, befide their inftantaneity.

Having ever made it my ambition to fee my writings diftinguifhed for fomething poignant, unexpected, or in fome refpects peculiar ; I have

acquired

acquired a degree of fame by a firm adherence to the Concetti. I have ftung folks with my epigrams, amufed them with acrofticks, puzzled them with rebufes, and diftracted them with riddles. It remained only for me to fucceed in the Impromptu, for which I was utterly difqualified by a whorefon flownefs of apprehenfion.

STILL defirous, however, of the immortal honour to grow diftinguifhed for an extempore, I petitioned Apollo to that purpofe in a dream. His anfwer was as follows, " That whatever " piece of wit, either written or verbal, makes " any pretence to merit, as of extemporaneous " production, fhall be faid or written within the " time that the author fupports himfelf on one " leg. That Horace had explained his mean- " ing, by the phrafe STANS PEDE IN UNO. " And forafmuch as one man may perfevere in " the pofture longer than another, he would re- " commend it to all candidates for this extraor- " dinary accomplifhment, that they would habi- " tuate themfelves to ftudy in no other attitude " whatfoever."

METHOUGHT I received his anfwer with the utmoft pleafure as well as veneration ; hoping that, however I was debarred of the acumen requifite for an extempore, I might learn to weary out my betters in ftanding on one leg.

AN

An HUMOURIST.

TO form an eftimate of the proportion which one man's happinefs bears to another's, we are to confider the mind that is allotted him with as much attenticn as the circumftances. It were fuperfluous to evince, that the fame objects which one defpifes, are frequently to another the fubftantial fource of admiration. The man of bufinefs and the man of pleafure are to each o- ther mutually contemptible, and a blue garter has lefs charms for fome, than they can difcover in a butterfly. The more candid and fage ob- ferver condemns neither for his purfuits, but for the derifion he fo profufely lavifhes upon the dif- pofition of his neighbour. He concludes, that fchemes infinitely various were at firft intended for our purfuit and pleafure ; and that fome find their account in heading a cry of hounds, as much as others in the dignity of Lord Chief Juftice.

HAVING premifed this much, I proceed to give fome account of a character which came within the fphere of my own obfervation.

NOT the entrance of a cathedral, not the found of a paffing bell, not the furs of a magi- ftrate, nor the fables of a funeral were fraught with half the folemnity of face !

NAY fo wonderfully ferious was he obferved to be on all occafions, that it was found hardly poffible to be otherwife in his company. He quafhed the loudeft tempeft of laughter, when-

ever

ever he entered the room, and mens features though ever fo much roughened, were fure to grow fmooth at his approach.

THE man had nothing vitious, or even ill-natured in his character ; yet he was the dread of all jovial converfation ; the young, the gay found their fpirits fly before him. Even the kitten and the puppy, as it were by inftinct, would forego their frolics, and be ftill. The depreffion he occafioned was like that of a damp, or vitiated air. Unconfcious of any apparent caufe, you found your fpirits fink infenfibly : And were any one to fit for the picture of ill-luck, it is not poffible the painter could felect a more proper perfon.

YET he did not fail to boaft of a fuperiour fhare of reafon, even for the want of that very faculty, rifibility, with which it is fuppofed to be always joined.

INDEED he acquired the character of the moft ingenious perfon of his county, from this meditative temper. Not that he had ever made any great difcovery of his talents ; but a few oracular declarations, joined with a common opinion that he was writing fomewhat for pofterity, completed his reputation.

NUMBERS would have willingly depretiated his character, had not his known fobriety and reputed fenfe deterred them.

HE was one day overheard at his devotions, returning his moft fervent thanks for fome particularities in his fituation, which the generality of mankind would have but little regarded.

Accept, faid he, the gratitude of thy moft humble, yet moft happy creature, not for filver or gold, the tinfel of mankind, but for thofe amiable peculiarities which thou haft fo gracioufly interwoven both with my fortune and my complexion; for thofe treafures fo well adapted to that frame of mind thou haft affigned me.

That the furname which has defcended to me is liable to no pun.

That it runs chiefly upon vowels and liquids.

That I have a picturefque countenance, rather than one that is efteemed of regular features.

That there is an intermediate hill, intercepting my view of a nobleman's feat, whofe ill-obtained fuperiority I cannot bear to recollect.

That my eftate is over-run with brambles, refounds with cataracts, and is beautifully varied with rocks and precipices, rather than an even cultivated fpot, fertile of corn, or wine, or oil; or thofe kinds of productions in which the fons of men delight themfelves.

That as thou divideft thy bounties impartially; giving riches to one, and the contempt of riches to another; fo thou haft given me, in the midft of poverty, to defpife the infolence of riches, and by declining all emulation that is founded upon wealth, to maintain the dignity and fuperiority of the mufes.

That I have a difpofition either fo elevated or fo ingenuous, that I can derive to myfelf amufement from the very expedients and contri-
vances

vances with which rigorous neceffity furnifhes my invention.

THAT I can laugh at my own follies, foibles, and infirmities ; and that I do not want infirmities to employ this difpofition.

THIS poor gentleman caught cold one winter's night, as he was contemplating, by the fide of a cryftal ftream, by moonfhine. This afterwards terminated in a fever that was fatal to him. Since his death I have been favoured with the infpection of his poetry, of which I preferved a catalogue for the benefit of my readers.

OCCASIONAL POEMS.

ON his dog, that growing corpulent refufed a cruft when it was offered him.

To the memory of a pair of breeches that had done him excellent fervice.

HAVING loft his trufty walking-ftaff, he complaineth.

To his miftrefs, on her declaring that fhe loved parfnips better than potatoes.

ON an ear-wig that crept into a nectarin that it might be fwallowed by Cloe.

ON cutting an artichoke in his garden, the day that Queen Anne cut her little finger.

EPIGRAM on a wooden-peg.

ODE to the memory of the great modern ⸺ who firft invented fhoe-buckles.

The HERMIT.

IN THE MANNER OF CAMBRAY.

'TWAS in that delightful month wlich Love prefers before all others, and wlich moſt reveres his deity ; that month which ever weaves a verdant carpet 'for the earth, and embroiders it with flowers. The banks became inviting through their coverlets of moſs : the violets, refreſhed by the moiſture of deſcending rains, enriched the tepid air with their agreeable perfumes. But the ſhower was paſt ; the ſun diſperſed the vapours ; and the ſky was clear and lucid, when Polydore walked forth. He was of a complexion altogether plain and unaffected; a lover of the Muſes, and beloved by them. He would oftentimes retire from the noiſe of mxed converſation, to enjoy the melody of birds, or the murmurs of a water-fall. His neighbours often ſmiled at his peculiarity of temper ; and he no leſs, at the vulgar caſt of theirs. He could never be content to paſs his irrevocable time in an idle comment upon a news-papei, or in adjuſting the preciſe difference of temperature betwixt the weather of to-day and yeſterlay. In ſhort, he was not void of ſome ambition, but what he felt he acknowledged, and was never averſe to vindicate. As he never cenſured any one who indulged their humour inoffenſively, ſo he claimed no manner of applauſe for thoſe purſuits which gratified his own. But the ſentiments

he

he entertained of honour, and the dignity conferred by royal authority, made it wonderful how he bore the thoughts of obfcurity and oblivion. He mentioned with applaufe the youth's who by merit had arrived at ftation ; but he thought that all fhould in life's vifit leave fome token of their exiftence, and that their friends might more reafonably expect it from them, than they from their pofterity.

THERE were few, he thought, of talents fo very inconfiderable, as to be unalterably excluded from all degrees of fame : and in regard to fuch as had a liberal education, he ever wifhed that in fome art or fcience they would be perfuaded to engrave their names. He thought it might be fome pleafure to reflect, that their names would at leaft be honoured by their defcendents, although they might efcape the notice of fuch as were not prejudiced in their favour.

WHAT a luftre, faid he, does the reputation of a Wren, a Waller, or a Walfingham, caft upon their remoteft progeny ? and who would not wifh rather to be defcended from them, than from the mere carcafe of nobility ? Yet where-ever fuperb titles are faithfully offered as the reward of merit, he thought the allurements of ambition were too tranfporting to be refifted. But to return.

POLYDORE, a new inhabitant in a fort of wild uninhabited country, was now afcended to the top of a mountain, and in the full enjoyment of a very extenfive profpect. Before him a broad and winding valley, variegated with all the charms of

of landscape ; fertile meadows, glittering streams,
pendent rocks, and nodding ruins. But these indeed were much less the objects of his attention,
than those distant hills and spires that were almost concealed by one undistinguished azure.
The sea indeed appeared to close the scene, tho',
distant as it was, it but little variegated the view;
Hardly indeed were it distinguishable but for the
beams of a descending sun, which at the same
time warned our traveller to return, before the
duskiness and dews of evening had rendered his
walk uncomfortable.

HE had now descended to the foot of the
mountain, when he remarked an old hermit approaching to a little hut, which he had formed
with his own hands, at the very bottom of the
precipice. Polydore, all enamoured of the beauties he had been surveying, could not avoid wondering at his conduct, who, not content with
shunning all commerce with mankind, had contrived as much as possible to exclude all views of
nature. He accosted him in the manner following. Father, says he, it is with no small surprise
that I observe your choice of situation, by which
you seem to neglect the most distant and delightful landscape that ever my eyes beheld. The hill
beneath which you have contrived to hide your
habitation, which would have afforded you such
a variety of natural curiosities, as to a person so
contemplative must appear highly entertaining :
and as the cell to which you are advancing is
seemingly of your own contrivance, methinks it

was

was probable you would have so placed it, as to present them, in all their beauty, to your eye.

The Hermit made him this answer. My son, says he, the evening approaches, and you have deviated from your way. I would not therefore detain you by my story, did I not imagine the moon would prove a safer guide to you, than that setting sun which you must otherwise rely upon. Enter therefore for a while into my cave, and I will give you then some account of my adventures, which will solve your doubts perhaps more effectually than any method I can propose. But before you enter my lone abode, calculated only for the use of meditation, dare to contemn superfluous magnificence, and render thyself worthy of the being I contemplate.

Know then, that I owe what the world is pleased to call my ruin (and indeed justly, were it not for the use which I have made of it) to an assured dependence, in a literal sense, upon confused and distant prospects : a consideration, which hath so indeed affected me, that I shall never henceforth enjoy a landscape that lies at so remote a distance as not to exhibit all its parts. And indeed were I to form the least pretensions to what your world calls taste, I might even then perhaps contend that a well-discriminated landscape was at all times to be preferred to a distant and promiscuous azure.

I was born in the parish of a nobleman who arrived to the principal management of the business of the nation. The heir of his family and myself were of the same age, and for some time
school-

school-fellows. I had made confiderable advances in his efteem, and the mutual affection
we entertained for each other, did not long remain
unobferved by his family or my own. He was
fent early upon his travels, purfuant to a very
injudicious cuftom, and my parents were folicited to confent that I might accompany him. Intimations were given to my friends, that a perfon of fuch importance as his father might contribute much more to my immediate promotion,
than the utmoft diligence I could ufe in purfuit
of it. My father, I remember, affented with
reluctance : my mother, fired with the ambition
of her fon's future greatnefs, through much im-
portunity " wrung from him his flow leave."
I, for my own part, wanted no great perfuafion.
We made what is called the greater tour of Europe. We neither of us, I believe, could be faid
to want natural fenfe, but being banifhed fo early in life, were more attentive to every deviation
from our own indifferent cuftoms, than to any
ufeful examination of their policies or manners.
Judgment, for the moft part, ripens very flowly.
Fancy often expands her bloffoms all at once.

WE were now returning home from a fix
years abfence ; anticipating the careffes of our
parents and relations, when my ever-honoured
companion was attacked by a fever. All poffible
means of fafety proving finally ineffectual, he
accofted me in one of his lucid intervals as follows.

ALAS ! my Clytander ! my life, they tell me,
is of very fhort continuance. The next paroxyfm
of my fever will probably be conclufive.

THE

THE profpect of this fudden change does not allow me to fpeak the gratitude I owe thee; much lefs to reward the kindnefs on which it is fo juftly grounded. Thou knoweft I was fent away early from my parents, and the more rational part of my life has been paffed with thee alone. It cannot be but they will prove folicitous in their inquiries concerning me. Thy narrative will awake their tendernefs, and they cannot but conceive fome for their fon's companion and his friend. What I would hope is, that they will render thee fome fervices, in place of thofe their beloved fon intended thee, and which I can unfeignedly affert, would have been only bounded by my power. My dear companion! farewell. All other temporal enjoyments have I banifhed from my heart; but friendfhip lingers long, and it is with tears I fay farewell.——

MY concern was truly fo great, that, upon my arrival in my native country, it was not at all increafed by the confideration that the nobleman on whom my hopes depended, was removed from all his places. I waited on him; and he appeared fenfibly grieved that the friendfhip he had ever profeffed could now fo little avail me. He recommended me however to a friend of his that was then of the fuccefsful party, and who, he was affured, would, at his requeft, affift me to the utmoft of his power. I was now in the prime of life, which I effectually confumed upon the empty forms of court-attendance. Hopes arofe before me like bubbles upon a ftream; as quick fucceeding one another, as fuperficial and

as vain. Thus bufied in my purfuit, and reject-
ing the affiftance of cool examination, I found
the winter of life approaching, and nothing procured to fhelter or protect me when my fecond
patron died. A race of new ones appeared before me, and even yet kept my expectations in
play. I wifhed indeed I had retreated fooner,
but to retire at laft unrecompenfed, and when a
few months attendance might happen to prove
fuccefsful, was beyond all power of refolution.

However, after a few years more attendance,
diftributed in equal proportions upon each of
thefe new patrons, I at length obtained a place
of much trouble and fmall emolument. On the
acceptance of this, my eyes feemed open all at
once. I had no paffion remaining for the fplendour which was grown familiar to me, and for
fervility and confinement I entertained an utter
averfion. I officiated however for a few weeks
in my poft, wondering ftill more and more how
I could ever covet the life I led. I was ever moft
fincere, but fincerity clafhed with my fituation
every moment of the day. In fhort, I returned
home to a fmall paternal income, not indeed in-
tending that auftere life in which you at prefent
find me engaged. I thought to content myfelf
with common neceffaries, and to give the reft,
if aught remained, to charity, but to avoid all
appearance of fingularity. But alas ! to my
great furprife, the perfon who fupplied my ex-
penfes, had fo far embroiled my little affairs,
that, when my debts, &c. were difcharged, I
was unable to fubfift in any better manner than

I

I do at prefent. I grew at firft entirely melancholy ; left the country where I was born, and raifed the humble roof that covers me in a country where I am not known. I now begin to think myfelf happy in my prefent way of life : I cultivate a few vegetables to fupport me, and the little well there is a very clear one. I am now an ufelefs individual ; little able to benefit mankind ; but a prey to fhame and to confufion, on the firft glance of every eye that knows me. My fpirits are indeed fomething raifed by a clear fky, or a meridian fun ; but as to extenfive views of the country, I think them well enough exchanged for the warmth and comfort which this vale affords me. Eafe is at leaft the proper ambition of age, and it is confeffedly my fupreme one.

YET will I not permit you to depart from an hermit without one inftructive leffon. Whatever fituation in life you ever wifh or propofe for yourfelf, acquire a clear and lucid idea of the inconveniencies attending it. I utterly contemned and rejected, after a month's experience, the very poft I had all my life-time been folicitous to procure.

C

On

On Diftinctions, Orders, and Dignities.

THE fubject turned upon the nature of focieties, ranks, orders, and diftinctions,
amongft men.

A GENTLEMAN of fpirit, and of the popular
faction, had been long declaiming againft any
kind of honours that tended to elevate a body
of people into a diftinct fpecies from the reft of
the nation. Particularly titles and blue ribands
were the object of his indignation. They were,
as he pretended, too invidious an oftentation of
fuperiority, to be allowed in any nation that
ftyled itfelf free. Much was faid upon the
fubject of appearances fo far as they were
countenanced by law or cuftom. The bifhop's lawn; the marfhal's truncheon; the baron's robe; and the judge's peruke, were confidered only as neceffary fubftitutes, where genuine purity, real courage, native dignity, and
fuitable penetration were wanting to complete
the characters of thofe to whom they were affigned.

IT was urged that policy had often effectually
made it a point to dazzle in order to enflave;
and inftances were brought of groundlefs diftinctions borne about in the glare of day by certain perfons, who, being ftripped of them,
would be lefs efteemed than the meaneft plebeian.

HE acknowledged, indeed, that kings, the
fountains of all political honour, had hitherto
fhewn

shewn no complaisance to that sex, whose softer dispositions rendered them more excusably fond of such peculiarities.

THAT in favour of the ladies, he should esteem himself sufficiently happy in the honour of inventing one order, which should be styled *The most powerful order of beauties.*

THAT their number in Great Britain should be limited to five thousand ; the dignity for ever to be conferred by the Queen alone, who should be styled sovereign of the order, and the rest the companions.

THAT the installment should be rendered a thousand times more ceremonious, the dresses more superb, and the plumes more enormous, than those already in use amongst the companions of the Garter.

THAT the distinguishing badge of this order should be an artificial nosegay ; to be worn on the left breast, consisting of a lily and a rose, the proper emblems of complexion, and intermixed with a branch of myrtle, the tree sacred to Venus.

THAT, instead of their shields being affixed to the stalls appointed for this order, there should be a gallery erected to receive their pictures at full length. Their portraits to be taken by four painters of the greatest eminence, and he whose painting was preferred, to be styled *A knight of the rose and lily.*

THAT when any person addressed a letter to a lady of this order, the style should always be *To the Right Beautiful Miss or Lady such-a-one.*

HE

He feemed for fome time undetermined whether they fhould forfeit their title upon marriage ; but at length, for many reafons, propofed it fhould be continued to them.

And thus far the gentleman proceeded in his harangue ; when it was objected, that the Queen, unlefs fhe unaccountably chofe to mark out game for her hufband, could take no fort of pleafure in conferring this honour where it was moft due : That as ladies grew in years, this epithet of beautiful would burlefque them ; and, in fhort, that, confidering the frailty of beauty, there was no lafting compliment that could be beftowed upon it.

At this the orator fmiled ; and acknowledged it was true : but afked, at the fame time, why it was more abfurd to ftyle a lady Right Beautiful, in the days of her deformity, than to term a peer Right Honourable when he grew a fcandal to mankind ?

That this was fometimes the cafe, he faid, was not to be difputed ; becaufe titles have been fometimes granted to a worthlefs fon, in confequence of a father's enormous wealth moft unjuftly acquired, And few had ever furpaffed in villany the Right Honourable the Earl of A——.

The company was a little furprifed at the fophiftry of our declaimant. However, it was replied to, by a perfon prefent, that Lord A——'s title being fictitious, no one ought to inftance him to the difadvantage of the p—rage, who had, ftrictly fpeaking, never been of that number.

On

On the fame Subject.

THE declaimant I before mentioned, continued his harangue. There are, faid he, certain epithets which fo frequently occur, that they are the lefs confidered ; and which are feldom or never examined, on account of the many opportunities of examination. that prefent themfelves.

Of this kind is the word *gentleman*. This word, on its firft introduction, was given, I fuppofe, to freemen in oppofition to vaffals ; thefe being the two claffes into which the nation was once divided *. The freeman was he, who was poffeffed of land, and could therefore fubfift without manual labour ; the vaffal, he, who tenanted the land, and was obliged to his thane for the neceffaries of life. The different-manners, we may prefume, that fprung from their different fituations and connections, occafioned the one to be, denominated a civilized or gentle perfonage ; and the other to obtain the name of a mere ruftic or villain.

BUT upon the publication of crufades, the ftate of things was confiderably altered. It was then that every freeman diftinguifhed the fhield which he wore with fome painted emblem or device ; and this, in order that his fellow-comba-

---

* As the author is not writing a treatife on the feudal law, but a moral effay, any little inaccuracies, it is to be hoped, will be overlooked by thofe, who, from feveral late treatifes on this fubject, might expect great exactnefs and precifion in a ferious difcuffion of this point.

tants might attribute to him his proper applaufe, which, upon account of fimilar accoutrements, might be otherwife fubject to mifapplication

Upon this there arofe a diftinction betwixt freeman and freeman. All which had ferved in thofe religious wars continued the ufe of their firft devices, but all devices were not illuftrated by the fame pretenfions to military glory.

However thefe campaigns were difcontinued: Frefh families fprung up; who, without any pretence to mark themfelves with fuch devices as thefe holy combatants, were yet as defirous of refpect, of eftimation, of diftinction. It would be tedious enough to trace the fteps by which money eftablifhes even abfurdity. A court of heraldry fprung up to fupply the place of crufade-exploits, to grant imaginary fhields and trophies to families that never wore real armour, and it is but of late that it has been difcovered to have no real jurifdiction.

Yet cuftom is not at once overthrown; and he is even now deemed a gentleman, who has arms recorded in the herald's office, and at the fame time follows none, except a liberal employment.

Allowing this diftinction, it is obvious to all who confider, that a churlifh, morofe, illiterate clown; a lazy, beggarly, fharping vagabond; a ftupid, lubberly, inactive fot, or pickpocket, nay even an highwayman, may be neverthelefs a gentleman as by law eftablifhed. In fhort, that the definition may, together with
others,

others, include alfo the filth, the fcum, and the dregs of the creation.

But do we not appear to difallow this account, when we fay " fuch or fuch an action " was not done in a gentleman-like manner?" " Such ufage was not the behaviour of a gentle- " man," and fo forth ? We feem thus to infinuate that the appellation of gentleman regards morals as well as family ; and that integrity, politenefs, generofity, and affability, have the trueft claim to a diftinction of this kind. Whence then fhall we fuppofe was derived this contradiction ? Shall we fay, that the plebeians, having the virtues on their fide, by degrees removed this appellation from the bafis of family to that of merit ; which they efteemed, and not unjuftly, to be the true and proper pedeftal ? This the gentry will fcarce allow. Shall we then infift that every thing great and god-like was heretofore the achievement of the gentry ? But this, perhaps, will not obtain the approbation of the commoners.

To reconcile the difference, let us fuppofe the denomination may belong equally to two forts of men. The one, what may be ftyled *a gentleman de jure*, viz. a man of generofity, politenefs, learning, tafte, genius, or affability ; in fhort, accomplifhed in all that is fplendid, or endeared to us by all that is amiable on the one fide ; and on the other, a gentleman *de facto*, or what, to Englifh readers, I would term a gentleman as by law eftablifhed.

As to the latter appellation, what is really effential,

fential, or, as logicians would fay, *quarto mo-do proprium*, is a real, or at leaft a fpecious claim to the inheritance of certain coat-armour from a fecond or more diftant anceftor ; and this unftained by any mechanical or illiberal em-ployment.

WE may difcover, on this ftate of the cafe, that, however material a difference this diftinc-tion fuppofes, yet it is not wholly impracticable for a gentleman *de jure*, to render himfelf in fome fort a gentleman *de facto*. A certain fum of money, depofited in the hands of my good friends Norroy or Rouge-dragon, will convey to him a coat of arms defcending from as many anceftors as he pleafes. On the other hand, the gentleman *de facto* may become a gentleman alfo *de jure*, by the acquifition of certain virtues; which are rarely all of them unattainable. The latter, I muft acknowledge, as the more difficult tafk ; at leaft, we may daily difcover, crouds acquire fufficient wealth to buy gentility, but very few that poffefs the virtues which ennoble human nature, and (in the beft fenfe of the word) conftitute a GENTLEMAN.

A

A CHARACTER.

—HE was a youth so amply furnished with every excellence of mind, that he seemed alike capable of acquiring or disregarding the goods of fortune. He had indeed all the learning and erudition that can be derived from universities, without the pedantry and ill manners which are too often their attendants. What few or none acquire by the most intense assiduity, he possessed by nature; I mean that elegance of taste, which disposed him to admire beauty under its great variety of appearances. It passed not unobserved by him either in the cut of a sleeve, or the integrity of a moral action. The proportion of a statue, the convenience of an edifice, the movement in a dance, and the complexion of a cheek or flower afforded him sensations of beauty; that beauty which inferiour geniuses are taught coldly to distinguish, or to discern rather than feel. He could trace the excellencies both of the courtier and the student; who are mutually ridiculous in the eyes of each other. He had nothing in his character that could obscure so great accomplishments, beside the want, the total want, of a desire to exhibit them. Through this it came to pass, that what would have raised another to the heights of reputation, was oftentimes in him passed over unregarded. For, in respect to ordinary observers, it is requisite to lay some stress yourself, on what you intend should be remarked by others; and this never was his way. His knowledge of books had in some degree diminished

minifhed his knowledge of the world; or, rather, the external forms and manners of it. His
ordinary converfation was, perhaps, rather too
pregnant with fentiment, the ufual fault of rigid
ftudents; and this he would in fome degree have
regulated better, did not the univerfality of his
genius, together with the method of his education, fo largely contribute to this amiable defect.
This kind of awkwardnefs (fince his modefty
will allow it no better name) may be compared to the ftiffnefs of a fine piece of brocade,
whofe turgefcency indeed conftitutes, and is in-
feparable from its value. He gave delight by an
happy boldnefs in the extirpation of common prejudices; which he could as readily penetrate, as
he could humoroufly ridicule : and he had fuch
entire poffeffion of the hearts, as well as under-
ftandlings of his friends, that he could foon make
the moft furprifing paradoxes believed and well-
accepted. His image, like that of a fovereign,
could give an additional value to the moft pre-
cious ore; and we no fooner believed our eyes,
that it was he who fpake it, than we as readily
believed whatever he had to fay. In this he dif-
fered from W——r, that he had the talents of
rendering the greateft virtues unenvied : whereas the latter fhone more remarkably in making his
very faults agreeable; I mean in regard to thofe
few he had to exercife his fkill.

N. B. This was written, in an extempore man-
    ner, on my friend's wall at Oxford, with a
    black lead pencil, 1735, and intended for his
    character.

O N

ON RESERVE.

A FRAGMENT.

T AK.I N G an evening's walk with a friend
in the country, among many grave remarks, he was making the following obfervation. There is not, fays he, any one quality fo
inconfiftent with refpect, as what is commonly called familiarity. You do not find one in
fifty whofe regard is proof againft it. At the
fame time it is hardly poffible to infift upon
fuch a deference as will render you ridiculous, if
it be fupported by common fenfe. Thus much
at leaft is evident, that your demands will be fo
fuccefsful, as to procure a greater fhare than if
you had made no fuch demand. I may frankly
own to you, Leander, that I frequently derived
uneafinefs from a familiarity with fuch perfons
as defpifed every thing they could obtain with
eafe. Were it not better, therefore, to be fomewhat frugal of our affability, at leaft to allot it
only to the few perfons of difcernment who can
make the proper diftinction betwixt real dignity and pretended : to neglect thofe characters,
which, being impatient to grow familiar, are at
the fame time very far from familiarity-proof :
to have pofthumous fame in view, which affords
us the moft pleafing landfcape : to enjoy the a-
mufement of reading, and the confcioufnefs that
reading paves the way to general efteem : to preferve

ferve a conftant regularity of temper, and alfo of conftitution, for the moft part but little confiftent with a promifcuous intercourfe with men : to fhun all illiterate, though ever fo jovial affemblies, infipid, perhaps, when prefent, and upon reflection painful : to meditate on thofe abfent or departed friends, who value or valued us for thofe qualities with which they were beft acquainted : to partake with fuch a friend as you, the delights of a ftudious and rational retirement. —— Are not thefe the paths that lead to happinefs ?

In anfwer to this (for he feemed to feel fome late mortification) I obferved, that what we loft by familiarity in refpect, was generally made up to us by the affection it procured ; and that an abfolute folitude was fo very contrary to our natures, that were he excluded from fociety, but for a fingle fortnight, he would be exhilarated at the fight of the firft beggar that he faw.

. WHAT follows were thoughts thrown out in our further difcourfe upon the fubject ; without order or connection, as they occur to my remembrance.

SOME referve is a debt to prudence ; as freedom and fimplicity of converfation is a debt to good nature.

THERE would not be any abfolute neceffity for referve, if the world were honeft : yet even then it would prove expedient. For in order to attain any degree of deference, it feems neceffary that people fhould imagine you have more accomplifhments than you difcover.

IT

IT is on this depends one of the excellencies of the judicious Virgil. He leaves you something ever to imagine : and such is the constitution of the human mind, that we think so highly of nothing, as of that whereof we do not see the bounds. This, as Mr Burke ingeniously observes, affords the pleasure when we survey a cylinder *. And Sir John Suckling says,

They who know all the wealth they have, are poor;
He's only rich who cannot tell his store.

A PERSON that would secure to himself great deference, will, perhaps, gain his point by silence, as effectually as by any thing he can say.

To be, however, a niggard of one's observations, is so much worse than to hoard up one's money, as the former may be both imparted and retained at the same time.

MEN oftentimes pretend to proportion their respect to real desert; but a supercilious reserve and distance wearies them into a compliance with more. This appears so very manifest to many persons of the lofty character, that they use no better means to acquire respect than like highwaymen to make a demand of it. They will, like Empedocles, jump into the fire, rather than betray the mortal part of their character.

IT is from the same principle of distance that nations are brought to believe that their great duke knoweth all things; as is the case in some countries.

* Treatise of the sublime and beautiful.

Men,

Men, while no human form or fault they see,
Excuse the want of ev'n humanity;
And eastern kings, who vulgar view disdain,
Require no worth to fix their awful reign.
You cannot say in truth what may disgrace 'em,
You know in what predicament to place 'em.
Alas ! in all the glare of light reveal'd,
Ev'n virtue charms us less than vice conceal'd!
For some small worth he had, the man was priz'd,
He added frankness---and he grew despis'd.

We want comets, not ordinary planets :

" *Taedet quotidianarum harum formarum.*"

TERENCE.

Hunc coelum, et stellas, et decedentia certis
Tempora momentis, sunt qui formidine nulla, imbuti
   spectent.

VIRTUES, like essences, lose their fragrance when exposed. They are sensitive plants which will not bear too familiar approaches.

LET us be careful to distinguish modesty, which is ever amiable, from reserve, which is only prudent. A man is hated sometimes for pride, when it was an excess of humility gave the occasion.

WHAT is often termed shiness, is nothing more than refined sense, and an indifference to common observations.

THE reserved man's intimate acquaintance are, for the most part, fonder of him, than the persons

fons of a more affable character, *i. e.* he pays them a greater compliment, than the other can do his, as he diftinguifhes them more.

It is indolence, and the pain of being upon one's guard, that makes one hate an artful character.

The moft referved of men, that will not exchange two fyllables together in an Englifh coffeehoufe, fhould they meet at Ifpahan, would drink fherbet, and eat a mefs of rice together.

The man of fhew is vain : the referved man is proud more properly. The one has greater depth, the other a more lively imagination.—The one is more frequently refpected, the other more generally beloved. The one a Cato; the other a Cæfar. *Vide* Salluft.

What Cæfar faid of *Rubicundos amo ; pallidos timeo ;* may be applied to familiarity, and to referve.

A reserved man often makes it a rule to leave company with a good fpeech : and I believe fometimes proceeds fo far as to leave company, becaufe he has made one. Yet it is his fate often, like the mole, to imagine himfelf deep when he is near the furface.

Were it prudent to decline this referve, and this horrour of difclofing foibles ; to give up a part of character to fecure the reft ? The world will certainly infift upon having fome part to pull to pieces, Let us throw out fome follies to the envious : As we give up counters to an highwayman, or a barrel to a whale, in order to fave one's money and one's fhip : To let it make ex-

ceptions

ceptions to one's head of hair, if one can escape being stabbed in the heart.

THE reserved man should drink double glasses.

PRUDENT men lock up their motives, letting familiars have a key to their heart, or to their garden.

A RESERVED man is in continual conflict with the social part of his nature; and even grudges himself the laugh into which he sometimes is betrayed.

Seldom he smiles——
And smiles in such a sort as he disdained
Himself——that could be moved to smile at any
    thing—

" A FOOL and his words are soon parted;" for so should the proverb run.

COMMON understandings, like cits in gardening, allow no shades to their picture.

MODESTY often passes for errant haughtiness; as what is deemed spirit in an horse proceeds from fear.

THE higher character a person supports, the more he should regard his minutest actions.

THE reserved man should bring a certificate of his honesty before he be admitted into company.

RESERVE is no more essentially connected with understanding, than a church-organ with devotion, or wine with good-nature *.

* THESE were no other than a collection of hints, when I proposed to write a poetical essay on Reserve.

On

On EXTERNAL FIGURE.

THERE is a young gentleman in my parifh, who, on account of his fuperiour equipage, is efteemed univerfally more proud and more haughty than his neighbours. It is frequently hinted, that he is by no means entitled to fo fplendid an appearance, either by his birth, his ftation, or his fortune; and that it is, of confequence, mere pride that urges him to live beyond his rank, or renders him blind to the knowledge of it. With all this fondnefs for external fplendour, he is a moft affable and ingenious man; and for this reafon I am inclined to vindicate him, when thefe things are mentioned to his difadvantage.

In the firft place, it is by no means clear, that drefs and equipage are fure figns of pride. Where it is joined with a fupercilious behaviour, it becomes then a corroborative teftimony. But this is not always the cafe: The refinements of luxury in equipage or a table, are perhaps as often the gratifications of fancy, as the confequence of an ambition to furpafs and eclipfe our equals. Whoever thinks that tafte has nothing to do here, muft confine the expreffion to improper limits; affuredly imagination may find its account in them, wholly independent of worldly homage and confiderations more invidious.

In the warmth of friendfhip for this gentleman, I am fometimes prompted to go further. I infift, it is not birth or fortune only that give a perfon claim to a fplendid appearance; that it

D 3. may

may be conferred by other qualifications in which my friend is acknowledged to have a fhare.

I HAVE fometimes urged, that remarkable ingenuity, any great degree of merit in learning, arts, or fciences, are a more reafonable authority for a fplendid appearance than thofe which are commonly prefumed to be fo. That there is fomething more perfonal in this kind of advantages than in rank or fortune, will not be denied: and furely there ought to be fome proportion obferved betwixt the cafe and the thing inclofed. The propenfity of rich and worthlefs people to appear with a fplendour upon all occafions, puts one in mind of the country fhopkeeper, who gilds his boxes in order to be the receptacle of pitch or tobacco. It is not unlike the management at our theatres royal, where you fee a piece of candle honoured with a crown.

I HAVE generally confidered thofe as privileged people, who are able to fupport the character they affume. Thofe who are incapable of fhining, but by drefs, would do well to confider that the contraft betwixt them and their cloaths turns out much to their difadvantage. It is on this account I have fometimes obferved with pleafure fome noblemen of immenfe fortune to drefs exceedingly plain.

IF drefs be only allowable to perfons of family, it may then be confidered as a fort of family livery, and Jack the groom may with equal juftice pride himfelf upon the gaudy wardrobe his mafter gives him. Nay more—for a gentleman, before he hire a fervant, will require fome teftimony

mony of his merit; whereas the master challenges his own right to splendour, though possessed of no merit at all.

UPON my present scheme of dress, it may seem to answer some very good purposes. It is then established on the same foundation, as the judge's robe and the prelate's lawn. If dress were only authorised in men of ingenuity, we should find many aiming at the previous merit, in hopes of the subsequent distinction. The finery of an empty fellow would render him as ridiculous as a star and garter would one never knighted: and men would use as commendable a diligence to qualify themselves for a brocaded waistcoat, or a gold snuff-box, as they now do to procure themselves a right of investing their limbs in lawn or ermine. We should not esteem a man a coxcomb for his dress, till, by frequent conversation, we discovered a flaw in his title. If he was incapable of uttering a *bon mot*, the gold upon his coat would seem foreign to his circumstances. A man should not wear a French dress, till he could give an account of the best French authors; and should be versed in all the oriental languages, before he should presume to wear a diamond.

IT may be urged, that men of the greatest merit may not be able to shew it in their dress, on account of their slender income. But here it should be considered that another part of the world would find their equipage so much reduced by a sumptuary law of this nature, that a very moderate degree of splendour would distinguish diftinguifh them more than a greater does at prefent.

WHAT I propofe however upon the whole is, that men of merit fhould be allowed to drefs in proportion to it ; but this with the privilege of appearing plain, whenever they found an expediency in fo doing : As a nobleman lays afide this garter, when he fees no valuable confequence in the difcovery of his quality.

A CHARACTER.

Animae nil magnae laudis egentes.

THERE is an order of perfons in the world whofe thoughts never deviate from the common road; whatever events occur, whatever objects prefent themfelves, their obfervations are as uniform, as though they were the confequence of inftinct.   There is nothing places thefe men in a more infignificant point of light, than a comparifon of their ideas with the refinements of fome great genius.   I fhall only add, by way of reflection, that it is people of this ftamp, that, together with the foundeft health, often enjoy the greateft equanimity: their paffions, like dull fteeds, being the leaft apt to endanger, or mifguide them: yet fuch is the fatality! Men of genius are often expected to act with moft difcretion, on account of that very fancy which is their greateft impediment.

I WAS taking a view of Weftminfter-abbey, with an old gentleman of exceeding honefty, but the fame degree of underftanding, as that I have defcribed.

THERE had nothing paffed in our way thither, befide the cuftomary falutations, and an endeavour to decide with accuracy upon the prefent temperature of the weather.   On paffing over the threfhold, he obferved with an air of thoughtfulnefs, that it was a brave ancient place.

I TOLD him, I thought there was none more fuitable,

fuitable, to moralize upon the futility of all earthly glory, as there was none which contained the afhes of men that had acquired a greater fhare of it. On this he gave a nod of approbation, but did not feem to comprehend me.

SILENCE enfued for many minutes; when having had time to reflect upon the monuments of men famous in their generations, he ftood collected in himfelf; affuring me, " there was no " fort of excellence could exempt a man from " death."

I APPLAUDED the juftice of his obfervation; and faid, it was not only my prefent opinion, but had been fo for a number of years. " Right," fays he, " and for my own part I feldom love to " publifh my remarks upon a fubject, till I have " had them confirmed to me by a long courfe of " experience."

THIS laft maxim, fomewhat beyond his ufual depth, occafioned a filence of fome few minutes. The fpring had been too much bent to recover immediately its wonted figure. We had taken fome few turns, up and down the left-hand ayle, when he caught fight of a monument fomewhat larger than the reft, and more calculated to make impreffion upon an ordinary imagination. As I remember, it was raifed to an anceftor of the D. of Newcaftle. " Well," fays he, with an air of cunning, " this is indeed a fine piece of work- " manfhip; but I cannot conceive this finery is " of any fignification to the perfon buried there." I told him, I thought not, and that, under a notion of refpect to the deceafed, people were

frequently

frequently impofed upon by their own pride and affectation.

WE were now arrived at the monument of Sir George Chamberlain; where my friend had juft perufed enough to inform him that he was an eminent phyfician, when he broke out with precipitation, and as though fome important dif-covery had ftruck his fancy on a fudden. I li-ftened to him with attention, till I found him la-bouring to infinuate that phyficians themfelves could not fave their lives when their time was come.

HE had not proceeded many fteps from it be-fore he beckoned to our Ciceroni. " Friend," fays he, pointing with his cane, " how long has " that gentleman been dead?" The man fet him right in that particular; after which putting on a woful countenance, " Well," fays he, " to be-" hold how faft time flies away! It is but a fmall " time to look back upon, fince he and I met at " the Devil *. Alas," continued he, " we fhall " never do fo again." Indulging myfelf with a pun that efcaped me on a fudden, I told him I hoped not; and immediately took my leave.

THIS old gentleman, as I have fince heard, paffed his life chiefly in the country; where it faintly participated either of pleafure or of pain. His chief delights indeed were fenfual, but thofe of the lefs vigorous kind, an afternoon's pipe, an evening-walk, or a nap after dinner. His death, which happened, it feems, quickly after, was occafioned by an uniform application to Bo-

* A well-known tavern near Temple-bar.

ftock's

stock's cordial, whatever his case required. Indeed his discourse, when any complained of sickness, was a little exuberant in the praises of this noble cathartic. But his distemper proving of a nature to which this remedy was wholly foreign, as well as this precluding the use of a more effectual recipe, he expired, not without the character of a most considerate person. I find by one part of his will, he obliged his heir to consume a certain quantity of ale among his neighbours, on the day he was born ; and by another, left a ring of bells to the church adjoining to his garden. It looks as if the old gentleman had not only an aversion to much reflection in himself, but endeavoured to provide against it in succeeding generations.

I HAVE heard that he sometimes boasted that he was a distant relation of Sir Roger de Coverly.

AN

An OPINION of GHOSTS.

IT is remarkable how much the belief of ghosts and apparitions of persons departed, has lost ground within these fifty years. This may perhaps be explained by the general growth of knowledge; and by the consequent decay of superstition, even in those kingdoms, where it is most essentially interwoven with their religion.

THE same credulity which disposed the mind to believe the miracles of a Popish saint, set aside at once the interposition of reason; and produced a fondness for the marvellous, which it was the priest's advantage to promote.

IT may be natural enough to suppose that a belief of this kind might spread in the days of Popish infatuation. A belief, as much supported by ignorance, as the ghosts themselves were indebted to the night.

BUT whence comes it that narratives of this kind have at any time been given by persons of veracity, of judgment, and of learning? Men neither liable to be deceived themselves, nor to be suspected of an inclination to deceive others, though it were their interest; nor who could be supposed to have any interest in it, even though it were their inclination.

HERE seems a further explanation wanting than what can be drawn from superstition.

I go upon a supposition, that the relations themselves were false. For as to the arguments sometimes ufed in this cafe, that had there been no true fhilling there had been no counterfeit, it feems wholly a piece of fophiftry. The true fhilling here, fhould mean the living perfon; and the counterfeit refemblance, the pofthumous figure of him, that either ftrikes our fenfes, or our imagination.

Supposing no ghoft then ever appeared, is it a confequence that no man could ever imagine that they faw the figure of a perfon deceafed? Snrely thofe who fay this, little know the force, the caprice, or the defects of the imagination.

Persons after a debauch of liquor, or under the influence of terrour, or in the deliria of a fever, or in a fit of lunacy, or even walking in their fleep, have had their brain as deeply impreffed with chimerical reprefentations, as they could poffibly have been, had thefe reprefentations ftruck their fenfes.

I have mentioned but a few inftances, wherein the brain is primarily affected. Others may be given, perhaps not quite fo common, where the ftronger paffions, either acute or chronical, have impreffed their object upon the brain; and this in fo lively a manner, as to leave the vifionary no room to doubt of their real prefence.

How difficult then muft it be to undeceive a perfon as to objects thus imprinted? Imprinted abfolutely with the fame force as their eyes themfelves could have pourtrayed them! And how many perfons muft there needs be, who could never be undeceived at all!

SOME

SOME of thefe caufes might not improbably have given rife to the notion of apparitions : and when the notion had been once promulgated, it had a natural tendency to produce more inftances.

The gloom of night, that was productive of terrour, would be naturally productive of apparitions. The event confirmed it.

THE paffion of grief for a departed friend, of horrour for a murdered enemy, of remorfe for a wronged teftator, of love for a miftrefs killed by inconftancy, of gratitude to a wife for long fidelity, of defire to be reconciled to one who died at variance, of impatience to vindicate what was falfely conftrued, of propenfity to confult with an advifer, that is loft.---The more faint as well as the more powerful paffions, when bearing relation to a perfon deceafed, have often, I fancy, with concurrent circumftances, been fufficient to exhibit the dead to the living.

BUT, what is more, there feems no other account that is adequate to the cafe as I have ftated it.   Allow this, and you have at once a reafon, why the moft upright may have publifhed a falfehood, and the moft judicious, confirmed an abfurdity.

SUPPOSING then that apparitions of this kind may have fome real ufe in God's moral government : is not any moral purpofe, for which they may be employed, as effectually anfwered on my fuppofition, as the other ? for furely it cannot be of any importance, by what means the brain receives thefe images. The effect, the conviction,

E 2   and

and the refolution confequent, may be juft the fame in either of the cafes.

Such appears, to me at leaft, to be the true exiftence of apparitions.

The reafons againft any external apparition, among others that may be brought, are thefe that follow.

They are, I think, never feen by day; and darknefs being the feafon of terrour and uncertainty, and the imagination lefs reftrained, they are never vifible to more than one perfon: which had more probably been the cafe, were not the vifion internal.

They have not been reported to have appeared thefe twenty years. What caufe can be affigned, were their exiftence real, for fo great a change as their difcontinuance?

The caufe of fuperftition has loft ground for this laft century; the notion of ghofts has been, together, exploded: A reafon why the imagination fhould be lefs prone to conceive them; but not a reafon why they themfelves fhould ceafe.

Most of thofe who relate that thefe fpectres have appeared to them, have been perfons either deeply fuperftitious in other refpects; of enthufiaftic imaginations, or ftrong paffions, which are the confequence; or elfe have allowedly felt fome perturbation at the time.

Some few inftances may be fuppofed, where the caprice of imagination, fo very remarkable in dreams, may have prefented fantafms to thofe that waked. I believe there are few but can recollect fome, wherein it has wrought miftakes

at

at leaft equal to that of a white-horfe for a winding fheet.

To conclude : As my hypothefis fuppofes
the chimera to give terrour equal to the reality,
our beft means of avoiding it, is to keep a ftrict
guard over our paffions——To avoid intempe-
rance, as we would a charnel-houfe; and by
making frequent appeals to cool reafon and common fenfe, fecure to ourfelves the property of a
well-regulated imagination.

ON CARDS.

**** WE had passed our evening with some certain persons famous for their taste, their learning, and refinement : but, as ill luck would have it, two fellows, duller than the rest, had contrived to put themselves upon a level by introducing A GAME AT CARDS.

'Tis a sign, said he, the world is far gone in absurdity, or surely the fashion of cards could be accounted no small one. Is it not surprising that men of sense should submit to join in this idle custom, which appears originally invented to supply its deficiency ? But such is the fatality ! imperfections give rise to fashions, and are followed by those who do not labour under the defects that introduced them. Nor is the hoop the only instance of a fashion invented by those who found their account in it, and afterwards countenanced by others to whose figure it was prejudicial.

How can men who value themselves upon their reflections, give encouragement to a practice which puts an end to thinking ?

I INTIMATED the old allusion of the bow that acquires fresh vigour by a temporary relaxation.

HE answered, this might be applicable, provided I could shew, that cards did not require the
pain

pain of thinking; and merely exclude from it, the profit and the pleafure.

CARDS, if one may guefs from their firft appearance, feem invented for the ufe of children; and, among the toys peculiar to infancy, the bells, the whiftle, the rattle, and the hobby-horfe, deferved their fhare of commendation. By degrees, men, who came neareft to children in underftanding, and want of ideas, grew enamoured of the ufe of them as a fuitable entertainment. Others alfo, pleafed to reflect on the innocent part of their lives, had recourfe to this amufement, as what recalled it to their minds. A knot of villains increafed the party; who, regardlefs of that entertainment which the former feemed to draw from cards, confidered them in a more ferious light, and made ufe of them as a more decent fubftitute to robbing on the road, or picking pockets. But men who propofe to themfelves a dignity of character, where will you find their inducement to this kind of game? For difficult indeed were it to determine, whether it appear more odious among fharpers, or more empty and ridiculous among perfons of character.

PERHAPS, replied I, your men of wit and fancy may favour this diverfion, as giving occafion for the crop of jeft and witticifm, which naturally enough arifes from the names and circumftances of the cards.

HE faid he would allow this as a proper motive, in cafe the men of wit and humour would accept the excufe themfelves.

IN

In fhort, fays he, as perfons of ability are capable of furnifhing out a much more agreeable entertainment, when a gentleman offers me cards, I fhall efteem it as his private opinion that I have neither fenfe nor fancy.

I asked how much he had loft---His anfwer was, he did not much regard ten pieces; but that it hurt him to have fquandered them away on cards; and that to the lofs of a converfation, for which he would have given twenty.

ON

ON HYPOCRISY.

WERE hypocrites to pretend to no uncommon fanctity, their want of merit would be lefs difcoverable. But pretenfions of this nature bring their characters upon the carpet. Thofe who endeavour to pafs for the lights of the world, muft expect to attract the eyes of it. A fmall blemifh is more eafily difcoverable in them, and more juftly ridiculous than a much greater in their neighbours. A fmall blemifh alfo prefents a clue, which very often conducts us through the moft intricate mazes, and dark receffes of their character.

NOTWITHSTANDING the evidence of this, how often do we fee pretence cultivated in proportion as virtue is neglected ! As religion finks in one fcale, pretence is exalted in the other.

PERHAPS there is not a more effectual key to the difcovery of hypocrify, than a cenforious temper. The man poffeffed of real virtue, knows the difficulty of attaining it ; and is, of courfe, more inclined to pity others, who happen to fail in the purfuit. The hypocrite, on the other hand, having never trod the thorny path, is lefs induced to pity thofe who defert it for the flowery one. He expofes the unhappy victim without compunction, and even with a kind of triumph ; not confidering that vice is the proper object of compaffion ; or that propenfity to cenfure is almoft a worfe quality than any it can expofe.

CLELIA was born in England, of Romifh parents,

rents, about the time of the revolution. She feemed naturally framed for love, if you were to judge by her external beauties ; but if you build your opinion on her outward conduct, you would have deemed her as naturally averfe to it.   Nu- merous were the garçons of the polite and gal- lant nation, who endeavoured to overcome her prejudices, and to reconcile her manners to her form.   Perfons of rank, fortune, learning, wit, youth, and beauty fued to her ; nor had fhe any reafon to quarrel with love, for the fhapes in which he appeared before her. Yet in vain were all applications.   Religion was her only object ; and fhe feemed refolved to pafs her days in all the aufterities of the moft rigid convent.   To this purpofe fhe fought out an abbefs that pre- fided over a nunnery in Languedoc, a fmall com- munity, particularly remarkable for extraordi- nary inftances of felf-denial.   The abbefs herfelf exhibited a perfon, in which chaftity appeared indeed not very meritorious.   Her character was perfectly well known before fhe went to prefide over this little fociety.   Her virtues were indeed fuch as fhe thought moft convenient to her cir- cumftances.   Her fafts were the effect of ava- rice, and her devotions of the fpleen.   She con- fidered the cheapnefs of houfe-keeping, as the great reward of piety, and added profufenefs to the feven deadly fins.   She knew fackcloth to be cheaper than brocade, and afhes than fweet powder.

Her heart fympathized with every cup that was broken, and fhe inftituted a faft for each
domeftic

domeſtic misfortune. She had converted her larder into a ſtudy, and the greater part of her library conſiſted of manuals for faſting-days. By theſe arts, and this way of life, ſhe ſeemed to enjoy as great a freedom from inordinate deſires, as the perſons might be ſuppoſed to do who were favoured with her ſmiles, or her converſation.

To this lady was Clelia admitted, and after the year of probation aſſumed the veil.

Among many others who had ſolicited her notice, before ſhe became a member of this convent, was Leander, a young phyſician of great learning and ingenuity. His perſonal accompliſhments were at leaſt equal to thoſe of any of his rivals, and his paſſion was ſuperiour. He urged in his behalf all that wit, inſpired by fondneſs, and recommended by perſon, dreſs, and equipage, could inſinuate ; but in vain. She grew angry at ſolicitations with which ſhe reſolved never to comply, and which ſhe found ſo difficult to evade.

But Clelia now had aſſumed the veil, and Leander was the moſt miſerable of mortals. He had not ſo high an opinion of his fair-one's ſanctity and zeal as ſome other of her admirers : but he had a conviction of her beauty, and that altogether irreſiſtible. His extravagant paſſion had produced in him a jealouſy that was not eaſily eluded.

At regina dolos —
Quid non ſentit amor ?

Hf.

HE had obferved his miftrefs go more frequently to her confeffor, a young and blooming eccle-
fiaftic, than was, perhaps, neceffary for fo much
apparent purity, or, as he thought, confiftent
with it.   It was enough to put a lover on the
rack, and it had this effect upon Leander.   His
fufpicions were by no means leffened, when he
found the convent to which Clelia had given the
preference before all others, was one where this
young friar fupplied a confeffional chair.

IT happened that Leander was brought to the
abbefs in the capacity of a phyfician, and he had
once more opportunity offered him of beholding
Clelia through the grate.

SHE, quite fhocked at his appearance, burft
out into a fudden rage, inveighing bitterly againft
his prefumption, and calling loudly on the name
of the bleffed virgin and the holy friar.   The
convent was, in fhort, alarmed ; nor was Clelia
capable of being pacified till the good man was
called, in order to allay, by fuitable applications,
the emotions raifed by this unexpected inter-
view.

LEANDER grew daily more convinced, that it
was not only verbal communications which paffed between Clelia and the friar.   This, however, he did not think himfelf fully warranted
to difclofe, till an accident, of a fingular nature,
gave him an opportunity of receiving more ample
teftimony.

The confeffor had a favourite fpaniel, which
he had loft for fome time, and was informed at
length that he was killed, at a village in the neighbourhood,

bourhood, being evidently mad. The friar was
at firſt not much concerned ; but in a little time
recollected that the dog had ſnapped his fingers
the very day before his elopement. A phyſician's
advice was thought expedient on the occaſion,
and Leander was the next phyſician. He told
him with great franknefs, that no prefcription
he could write had the fanction of fo much experience as immerfion in fea-water. The friar,
therefore, the next day fet forward upon his
journey, while Leander, not without a miſchie-
vous kind of fatisfaction, conveys the following
lines to Clelia.

       " My charming CLELIA,

     " Though I yet love you to diſtraction, I can-
" not but fufpect that you have granted favours
" to your confeffor, which you might, with great-
" er innocence, have granted to Leander. All
" I have to add is this, that amorous intercour-
" fes of this nature, which you have enjoyed
" with Friar Laurence, put you under the like
" neceffity with him, of feeking a remedy in the
" ocean.

           " Adieu ! LEANDER !"

IMAGINE Clelia guilty, and then imagine her
confufion. To rail was infignificant, and to blame
her phyſician was abfurd, when fhe found herfelf under a neceffity of purfuing his advice.
The whole fociety was made acquainted with the
journey fhe was undertaking, and the caufes of
it. It were uncharitable to fuppofe the whole

VOL. II.   F   community

community únder the fame conftraint with the unhappy Clelia. However, the greater part thought it decent to attend her. Some went as her companions, fome for exercife, fome for a-mufement, and the abbefs herfelf as guardian of her train, and concerned in her fociety's mif-fortunes.

WHAT ufe Leander made of his difcovery, is not known. Perhaps when he had been fuccefs-ful in banifhing the hypocrite, he did not fhew himfelf very folicitous in his endeavours to re-form the finner.

N. B. Written when I went to be dipped in the falt water.

O N

On VANITY.

HISTORY preferves the memory of empires and of ftates, with which it neceffarily interweaves that of heroes, kings, and ftatefmen. Biography affords a place to the remarkable characters of private men. There are likewife other fubordinate teftimonies, which ferve to perpetuate, at leaft prolong, the memories of men, whofe characters and ftations give them no claim to a place in ftory. For inftance, when a perfon fails of making that figure in the world, which he makes in the eyes of his own relations or himfelf, he is rarely dignified any farther than with his picture whilft he is living, or with an infcription upon his monument after his deceafe. Infcriptions have been fo fallacious, that we begin to expect little from them befide elegance of ftyle. To inveigh againft the writers, for their manifeft want of truth, were as abfurd as to cenfure Homer for the beauties of an imaginary character. —— But even paintings, in order to gratify the vanity of the perfon who befpeaks them, are taught now-a-days to flatter like epitaphs.

FALSEHOODS upon a tomb or monument may be entitled to fome excufe in the affection, the gratitude, and piety of furviving friends. Even grief itfelf difpofes us to magnify the virtues of a relation, as vifible objects alfo appear larger through tears. But the man who through an idle vanity fuffers his features to be belied, or ex-

F 2   changed

changed for others of a more agreeable make, may with great truth be said to lose his property in the portrait. In like manner, if he encourage the painter to belie his dress, he seems to transfer his claim to the man with whose station his assumed trappings are connected.

I REMEMBER a bag-piper, whose physiognomy was so remarkable and familiar to a club he attended, that it was agreed to have his picture placed over their chimney-piece. There was this remarkable in the fellow, that he chose always to go barefoot, though he was daily offered a pair of shoes. However, when the painter had been so exact as to omit this little piece of dress, the fellow offered all he had in the world, the whole produce of three night's harmony, to have those feet covered in the effigie, which he so much scorned to cover in the original. Perhaps he thought it a disgrace to his instrument, to be eternized in the hands of so much apparent poverty. However, when a person of low station adorns himself with trophies to which he has no pretensions to aspire, he should consider the picture as actually telling a lie to posterity.

THE absurdity of this is evident, if a person assume to himself a mitre, a blue garter, or a coronet, improperly ; but station may be falsified by other decorations, as well as these.

BUT I am driven into this grave discourse on a subject, perhaps, not very important, by a real fit of spleen. I this morning saw a fellow drawn in a night-gown of so rich a stuff, that the expense, had he purchased such a one, would more

than

than half have ruined him ; and another cox-:
comb, feated by his painter in a velvet chair, who
would have been furprifed at the deference paid
him, had he been offered a cufhion.

——— *Gaudent praenomine molles*
Auriculae ———

IT is a very convenient piece of knowledge.
for a perfon upon a journey, to know the com-
pellations with which it is proper to addrefs thofe
he happens to meet by his way. Some accuracy
here may be of ufe to him who would be well
directed either in the length or the tendency of
his road ; or be freed from any itinerary difficulties incident to thofe who do not know the
country. It may not be indeed imprudent to ac-,
coft a paffenger with a title fuperiour to what
he may appear to claim. This will feldom fail
to diffufe a wonderful alacrity in his countenance;
and be, perhaps, a method of fecuring you from
any miftake of greater importance.

I was led into thefe obfervations by fome fo-
licitudes I lately underwent, on account of my
ignorance in thefe peculiarities. Being fomewhat more verfed in books, than I can pretend
to be in the orders of men, it was my fortune
to undertake a journey, which I was to perform
by means of inquiries. I had paffed a number
of miles without any fort of difficulty, by help
of the manifold inftructions that had been given
me on my fetting out. At length, being fomething dubious concerning my way, I met a perfon, whom, from his nightcap, and feveral do-

meftic

meſtic parts of dreſs, I deemed to be of the neighbourhood.   His ſtation of life appeared, to me,
to be what we call a gentleman-farmer; a ſort of
ſubaltern character ; in reſpect of which, the
world ſeems not invariably determined.   It is in
ſhort what King Charles the Second eſteemed the
happieſt of all ſtations ; ſuperiour to the toilſome
taſk and ridiculous dignity of conſtable ; and as
much inferiour to the intricate practice and invidious deciſions of a juſtice of peace.   " Honeſt
" man," ſays I, " be ſo good as to inform me
" whether I am in the way to Mirlington ? " He
replied, with a ſort of ſurlineſs, that he knew nothing of the matter ; and turned away with as
much diſguſt, as though I had called him rogue
or raſcal.

    I DID not readily penetrate the cauſe of his
diſpleaſure, but proceeded on my way with hopes,
to find other means of information.   The next
I met was a young fellow, dreſſed in all the pride
of rural ſpruceneſs ; and, beſide him, walked a
girl in a dreſs agreeable to that of her companion.   As I preſumed him by no means averſe
to appear conſiderable in the eyes of his miſtreſs,
I ſuppoſed a compliment might not be diſagree-
able ; and inquiring the road to Mirlington, ad-
dreſſed him by the name of " Honeſty."   The
fellow, whether to ſhow his wit before his miſtreſs, or whether he was diſpleaſed with my familiarity, I cannot tell, directed me to follow a
part of my face, (which I was well aſſured could
be no guide to me), and that other parts would
follow of conſequence.

                                    THE

THE next I met, appeared, by his look and gait, to ſtand high in his own opinion. I therefore judged the beſt way of proceeding was to adapt my phraſe to his own ideas, and ſaluting him by the name of *Sir*, deſired to obtain ſome inſight into my road. My gentleman, without heſitation, gave me ample inſtructions for the reſt of my journey.

I PASSED on, muſing with myſelf, why an appellation relative to fortune ſhould be preferred to one founded on merit ; when I happened to behold a gentleman examining a ſun-dial in his garden. " Friend," ſays I, " will you tell " me what a clock it is ?" He made me no ſort of anſwer, and ſeemed as much diſſatisfied with my openneſs of temper, as with the confidence I placed in his. — The refuſal of an anſwer in this caſe, was not of much importance. I proceeded on my way, and happened to meet a very old woman, whom I determined to accoſt by the appellation of *Dame* ; and withal wiſhed her a good night.

BUT, alas ! ſhe ſeemed ſo little pleaſed with the manner of my addreſs, that ſhe returned me no manner of thanks for my kind wiſhes as to her repoſe. It is not clear whether my phraſe was faulty, in regard to her dignity, or in reſpect of her age. But it is very probable ſhe might conclude it an impropriety in reſpect of both.

I HAD by this time found the inconvenience of an utter ignorance in rural diſtinctions. The future part of my journey afforded me yet further

ther means of conviction. I was expofed to the danger of three quickfands, by calling a girl *Sweetheart*, inftead of Madam ; and was within a foot of rufhing down a precipice, by calling another, *Forfooth*, who might eafily have told me how to avoid it.

In fhort, I found myfelf well or ill ufed, as I happened, or not, to fuit my falutations to people's ideas of their own rank. Towards the laft part of my ftage, I was to pafs a brook, fo much fwelled by land-floods, that the proper way through it was undiftinguifhable. A well-dreff- ed gentleman was pafling a bridge on my left hand. It was here of much importance for me to fucceed in my inquiry. I was, therefore, meditating within myfelf which might be the moft endearing of all appellations ; and at laft befought him to give me fome inftructions, un- der the name of *Honeft Friend.* He was not feemingly fo much pleafed, as I affured myfelf he would be, and trudged onward without re- ply. After this, I had not gone many fteps (out of the path, for fo it proved) before I found myfelf and horfe plunged headlong in the brook ; and my late honeft friend in a laughter at our downfall.

I made a fhift, however, to recover both my- felf and horfe, and, after a few more difficulties, arrived at the end of my journey. I have fince made ftrict inquiry into the due application of fuch inferiour titles, and may, perhaps, com- municate them to you, on fome future occafion. In the mean time, you may, if you pleafe, con-

fider

fider the vaſt importance of fuperiour titles,
when there is no one fo inconfiderable, but
there is alfo a mind that it can influence.

WHEN you reflect upon this fubject, you
will, perhaps, be lefs fevere on your friend ——
who, you tell me, is now trafficking for this
fpecies of dignity.

LEARN to be wife then from others harm;
and do not forget to obferve decorum, on every
occafion that you may have to addrefs him for
the future. Pretend no more at the clofe of
your epiftle to be his faithful fervant, much lefs
his affectionate one. Tender your fervices with
great refpect, if you do not chufe to do it with
profound veneration. He will certainly have no
more to do with fincerity and truth. Remember,

Male fi palpere, recalcitrat.

On.

On MODESTY and IMPUDENCE.

WHEN a man of genius does not print, he difcovers himfelf by nothing more than by his abilities in difpute. However let him fhew folidity in his opinions, together with eafe, elegance, and vivacity in his expreffions, yet if an impudent face be found to baffle him, he fhall be judged inferiour in other refpects. I mean he will grow cheap in mixed company : for as to felect judges, they will form their opinions by another fcale : with thefe, a fingle e-piftle, penned with propriety, will more effectual-ly prove his wit, than an hundred defects in his converfation will demonftrate the reverfe.

IT is true there is nothing difplays a genius, I mean a quicknefs of genius, more than a dif-pute ; as two diamonds, encountering, contri-bute to each other's luftre. But perhaps the odds is much againft the man of tafte in this particular.

BASHFULNESS is more frequently connected with good fenfe, than we find affurance : and impudence, on the other hand, is often the mere effect of downright ftupidity. On this ac-count the man of genius has as much the advan-tage of his antagonift, as a race-horfe, carrying a fmall weight, has over his rival that bears a larger ; modefty, like the weight to which I al-lude, not fuffering its owner to exert his real ftrength ; which effrontery is allowed to do, without let or impediment.

IT

It may be urged, and juftly enough, that it is common to be partial to the modeft man; and that diffidence makes good amends for any reftraint it lays us under, by the prejudice it gives every hearer in our favour. But indeed this can only happen, where it meets with the moft ingenuous judges. Otherwife a laugh will carry the day, with which the ignorant fide is generally beft accommodated.

In order to put thefe antagonifts upon a fomewhat more equal footing, I have invented the following inftrument; for the fole ftructure and fale of which, I am not without hopes of procuring a patent. What I mean, is an artificial laughter. There are few fo little converfant in toys, but muft have feen inftruments mechanically framed to counterfeit the voices of different birds. The quail-pipe is brought to fuch perfection as even to delude the very fpecies. The cuckow has been mimicked with no lefs accuracy. Would it not then be an eafy matter to reprefent the laugh of this empty tribe, which has in itfelf fomething artificial; and is not more affected than it is particular? For the convenience of the perfon that bears it, its dimenfions fhould be fo contrived as that it might be played on in his pocket. Does it not feem feafible, that a laughter of this kind may be brought to anfwer every purpofe of that noife which it refembles? If there be occafion for an expletive, let the owner feek it in his fobb; as his antagonift would find his account in a loud oath or an empty pun. If there be need of a good founding cadence at

the

the clofe of a common period, it may not be a-
mifs to harmonize a fentence by what may be called *a finifbing-ftroke.* This inftrument is fo contrived as to produce all the variety of an human
laugh ; and this variation is to be regulated, not
by the nature of your fubject, nor the wit or
humour of a repartee, but by the difpofition of
the company, and the proper minute for fuch
an interlude. But to become a mafter of the
faid machine, let the candidate for applaufe frequent the company of vociferous difputants ;
among whom he may foon learn how to perform a converfation.

ONE or two of thefe inftruments I have already finifhed, though not indeed to the perfection, at which I expect they may foon arrive. A
gentleman vifited me t'other day who has the
jufteft claim that can be, to the ufe of them ;
having nothing in his character that can obfcure
the greateft merit, but the greateft modefty. I
communicated my invention, defiring him to make
trial of it, on the firft occafion. He did fo, and
when I faw him next, gave me leave to publifh
the following account of its efficacy in my next
advertifement. The firft time I employed it, faid
my friend, was in a fort of controverfy with a
beau ; who had contrived means by the ufe of
his fnuff-box, to fupply both want of language
and of thought. In this manner he prolonged
his argument ; and really to the company, which
confifted of ladies, difcovered more fagacity without thinking, than I could do by its affiftance.
I bethought myfelf immediately of your inftru-

ment,

ment, and had recourfe to it. I obferved in what
part of his difcourfe he moft employed his fingers, and had fuddenly recourfe to mine, with
equal emphafis and fignificancy. The art was
not difcovered, ere I had routed my antagonift;
having feated myfelf in a dark corner, where my
operations were not difcernible. I obferved, that
as he found himfelf more clofely preffed, he grew
more and more affiduous in his application to his
fnuff-box, much as an otter clofely purfued is
forced to throw up bubbles that fhow his diftrefs.
I therefore difcovered gradually lefs and lefs occafion for fpeaking; and for thinking none at all.
I played only a flourifh in anfwer to the argument at his finger's ends; and after a while found
him as mortal in this part as in any other. When
his caufe was juft expiring, after a very long purfuit, and many fruitlefs turnings and evafions in
the courfe of it, I founded my inftrument with
as much alacrity, as a huntfman does his horn on
the death of an hare.

THE next whom I engaged was a more formidable difputant; and I own with a fenfe of gratitude that your inftrument alone could render
me a match for him. His ftrength of argument
was his ftrength of lungs; and he was, unqueftionably, an able antagonift. However, if your
machine put me upon a par with him, I think I
may fay without vanity, that, in point of reafon, I
had the upper hand. I fhall only add, that as it
was habitual for him to anfwer arguments by vo-
ciferation, fo it became needlefs for me to give
him any anfwer of a better kind.

Thus far my friend : I do not queſtion but there will appear artiſts, that ſhall undertake to inſtruct the diffident, the ſubmiſſive, and the baſhful, how to perform the whole gamut of oratorical and riſible muſic : and as there is a kind of humorous laughter, which draws all others into its own vortex, I need not here aſſert that I would have this branch very much inculcated.

NEITHER is this inſtrument of importance in diſpute alone, or controverſy ; but where-ever one man's faculties are more prone to laughter than another's.   Trifles will burſt one man's ſides, which will not diſturb the features of another ; and a laugh one cannot join, is almoſt as irkſome as a lamentation.   It is like a peal rung after a wedding ; where a whole pariſh ſhall be ſtunned with noiſe, becauſe they want that occaſion to rejoice, which the perſons at leaſt imagine to be their lot, that occaſioned it.   The ſounds are pleaſing to their ears, who find them conformable to their own ideas ; but thoſe who are not in temper, or unconcerned, find them a ſtupefying repetition.

WHEN therefore my mind is not in tune with another's, what ſtrikes his will not vibrate on mine.   All I then have to do, is to counterfeit a laugh ; which is an operation as artificial, as the machine I have been deſcribing.

THE actions of our lives, even thoſe we call moſt important, ſeem as much ſubject to trifles, as our very lives themſelves.   We frame many notable projects in imagination, and promiſe to ourſelves an equal term of life.   It is however

in

in the power of the minuteft accident, to fhorten
the one, and disconcert the other. It is with
mankind as with certain fire-engines, whofe motion may be ftopped in the midft of its rapidity,
by the interpofition of ftraw in a particular part
of them.

THE following tranflation from the original
Spanifh, will fufficiently illuftrate the foregoing
affertion. Dod Pedro * * * * was one of the
principal grandees of his age and country. He
had a genius equal to his birth, and a difpofition
remarkably contemplative. It was his cuftom,
on this account, to retire from the world at ftated periods, and to indulge himfelf in all the
mazes of a fine imagination. It happened as he
one day fat in his ftudy, that he fixed his eye on
a neighbouring fpider. The moft trivial object
(if any natural object can be termed fo) ferved
him frequently for the foundation of fome moral and fublime reflection. He furveyd the creature attentively, and indulged the bias of his
thought, till he was loft in the excurfions of a
profound reverie. The curious workmanfhip of
this unregarded animal brought at once into his
mind the whole art of fortification. He obferved the deficiency of human fkill, and that no
cunning could have contrived her fo proper an
habitation. He found that no violence could
affect the extremities of her lines, but what was
immediately perceptible, and liable to alarm her
at the centre. He obferved the road by which
fhe fallied forth, ferved to convey intelligence
from without, at the fame time that it added

G 2   ftrength

ftrength and ftability to the work within. He was at once furprifed and pleafed with an object, which, although common, he happened not to have beheld in the fame light, or with the fame attention. From this inftant he bent his thoughts upon the advancement of military fortification : and he often would declare it was this trivial incident that gave him a relifh for that ftudy, which he afterwards purfued with fuch application and fuccefs.

He fpent, in fhort, fo much time upon the attainment of this fcience, that he grew as capable of executing any part of it, as fpeculation alone could render him. Nothing wanted now, but practice, to complete the fame of his abilities. That in fhort was his next purfuit. He became defirous of experiencing what had been fo fuccefsful in imagination, and to make thofe mural fallies, which had been attended there with victory. To this end he had little to do, but excite the ambition of his young monarch ; to enforce by teftimony of his friends his qualifications for the poft he fought ; and, on the firft delivery of his petition, to obtain preferment from the king.

This happened to be a time of the profoundeft tranquility ; little agreeable to a perfon eager of glory, furnifhed with fkill, and confcious of abilities. Such was this ingenious nobleman. He well knew the ambition of princes, and of his monarch in particular. But he was not acquainted with his own. That imperious and fubtle paffion, is often moft predominant when it is leaft perceived. When it once prevails in any great
degree,

degree, we find our reafon grow fubfervient, and, inftead of checking or contradicting, it ftoops to flatter and to authorife it. Inftead of undeceiving, fhe confirms us in our errour ; and even levels the mounds and fmooths the obftructions, which it is her natural province to interpofe. This was the cafe of Don Pedro. The delicacy of his tafte increafed his fenfibility; and his fenfibility made him more a flave. The mind of man; like the finer parts of matter, the more delicate it is, naturally admits the more deep and the more vifible impreffions. The pureft fpirits are the fooneft apt to take the flame. Let us therefore be the more candid to him, on account of the vivacity of his paffions, feduced, as indeed he was, into very unwarrantable fchemes.

HE had in brief conceived a project, to give his mafter an univerfal monarchy, He had calculated every article, with the utmoft labour and precifion, and intended, within a few days, to prefent his project to the king.

SPAIN was then in a ftate of affluence ; had a large army on foot, together with means and opportunities of raifing an immenfe one. It were impoffible to anfwer for the poffible events, that might deftroy their hopes of fuch an enterprife. Difficulty often attends the execution of things the moft feafible and well-contrived in theory. But whoever was acquainted with the author of this project, knew the pofture of affairs in Europe at that time, the ambition of the prince, and the many circumftances that confpired to favour it, might have thought the project would have

been

been agreed to, put in practice, and, without fome particular interpofition of fortune, been attended with fuccefs.—But fortune did not put herfelf to any particular trouble about the matter.

DON PEDRO, big with vaft defigns, was one day walking in his fields. He was promifed the next morning an audience of the king. He was preparing himfelf for a converfation, which might prove of fo much confequence to all mankind; when walking thoughtfully along and regardlefs of his path, his foot happened to ftumble, and to overturn an ant's neft. He caft his eyes upon the ground to fee the occafion of his miftake, where he fpied the little animals in the moft miferable confufion. He had the delicacy of fentiment, to be really forry for what he had done; and, putting himfelf in their condition, began to reflect upon the confequence. It might be an age, to them, ere they could recover their tranquillity. He viewed them with a fort of fmile to find the anxiety they underwent for fuch perifhable habitations. Yet he confidered that his contempt was only the effect of his own fuperiority; and that there might be fome created beings to whom his own fpecies muft appear as trifling. His remark did not ceafe here. He confidered his future enterprife, with an eye to fuch a race of beings. He found it muft appear to them in a light as difadvantageous, as the ambition and vain-glory of an ant would, to himfelf. How ridiculous, he faid, muft this republic appear to me,

me, could I difcern its actions, as it has probably
many, that are analogous to thofe of human
nature? Suppofe them at continual variance a-
bout the property of a grain of fand. Suppofe
one, that had acquired a few fands more to his
portion — as alfo one grain of wheat, and one
fmall particle of barley-flour, fhould think himfelf qualified to tyrannize over his equals, and to
lord it uncontrolled. Confider him, on this account, not contented to make ufe of the numerous legs withwhich nature has fupplied him, borne
aloft by a couple of flaves within the hollow of
an hufk of wheat, five or fix others, at the fame
time, attending folemnly upon the proceffion.
Suppofe laftly, that, among this people, the prime
minifter fhould perfuade the reft to level war
upon a neighbouring colony; and this in order
to be ftyled the fovereign of two hillocks, inftead
of one; while perhaps their prefent condition
leaves them nothing to wifh befide fuperfluities.
At the fame time, it is in the power of the moft
inconfiderable among mankind, nay of any fpecies of animals fuperiour to their own, to deftroy
at once the minifter and the people altogether:
This is doubtlefs very ridiculous, yet this is doubtlefs my own cafe, in refpect of many fubordinate
beings, and very certainly of the fupreme one.
Farewell then ye air-built citadels! Farewell vi-
fions of unfolid glory! Don Pedro will feek no
honour of fo equivocal an acceptation, as to de-
grade his character to a fuperiour fpecies, in proportion as it exalts him before his own.

SEE

SEE here a juft conclufion ! In fhort, he found it fo fairly drawn, as immediately to drop his project, leave the army, and retire : of which whimfical relation it may be well enough obferved, that a fpider had enflaved the world had not an ant obftructed his defign.

UPON

UPON ENVY.

TO A FRIEND, R. G.

WHENCE is it, my friend, that I feel it impoſſible to envy you, although hereafter your qualifications may make whole millions do ſo ? for, believe me, when I affirm, that I deem it much more ſuperfluous, to wiſh you honours to gratify your ambition, than to wiſh you ambition enough, to make your honours ſatisfactory.

IT ſeems an hard caſe that envy ſhould be the conſequence of merit, at the ſame time that ſcorn ſo naturally attends the want of it. It is however in ſome meaſure perhaps unavoidable (and perhaps in ſome ſenſe an uſeful) paſſion in all the moſt heroic natures; where, refined through certain ſtrainers, it takes the name of emulation. It is a pain ariſing in our breaſts, on contemplation of the ſuperiour advantages of another : and its tendency is truly good, under ſome certain regulations.

ALL honour, very evidently, depends upon compariſon ; and conſequently the more numerous are our ſuperiours, the ſmaller portion of it falls to our ſhare. Conſidered relatively, we are dwarfs, or giants; though conſidered abſolutely, we are neither. However the love of this relative grandeur, is made a part of our natures ; and the uſe of emulation is to excite our diligence in

purſuit

purfuit of power, for the fake of beneficence. The inftances of its perverfion are obvious to every one's obfervation. A vitious mind, inftead of its own emolument, ftudies the debafement of his fuperiour. A perfon, to pleafe one of this caft, muft needs diveft himfelf of all ufeful qualities; and in order to be beloved, difcover nothing that is truly amiable. One may very fafely fix our efteem on thofe whom we hear fome people depretiate. Merit is to them as uni-- formly odious, as the fun itfelf to the birds of darknefs. An author, to judge of his own merit, may fix his eye upon this tribe of men; and fuffer his fatisfaction to arife in due proportion to their difcontent. Their difapprobation will fufficiently influence every generous bofom in his favour: and I would as implicitly give my applaufe to one whom they pull to pieces; as the inhabitants of Pegu worfhip thofe that have been devoured by apes.

'Tis another perverfion of this paffion, though of a lefs enormous nature, when it merely ftimulates us to rival others in points of no intrinfic worth. To equal others in the ufelefs parts of learning; to purfue riches for the fake of an equipage as brilliant; to covet an equal knowledge of a table; to vie in jockeyfhip, or cunning at a bett. Thefe and many other rivalfhips, anfwer not the genuine purpofes of emulation.

I believe the paffion is oftentimes derived from a too partial view of our own and others excellencies. We behold a man poffeffed of fome particular advantage, and we immediately reflect
upon

upon its deficiency in ourfelves. We wait not to examine what others we have to balance it. We envy another man's bodily acomplifhments; when our mental ones might preponderate, would we put them into the fcale. Should we afk our own bofoms whether we would change fituations altogether, I fancy felf-love would, generally, make us prefer our own condition. But if our fentiments remain the fame after fuch an examination, all we can juftly endeavour is our own real advancement. To meditate his detriment either in fortune, power, or reputation, at the fame time that it is infamous, has often a tendency to deprefs ourfelves. But let us confine our emulation to points of real worth; to riches, power, or knowledge; only that we may rival others in beneficence.

A

A VISION.

INGENIOUS was the device of those celebrated
worthies, who, for the more effectual pro-
mulgation of their well-grounded maxims, first
pretended to divine inspiration. Peace be to their
manes; may the turf lie lightly on their breast;
and the verdure over their grave, be as perpe-
tual as their memories! Well knew they, que-
stionless, that a proceeding of this nature, must
afford an excuse to their modesty, as well as add
a weight to their instructions. For, from the
beginning of time, if we may believe the histories
of the best repute, man has ever found a delight
in giving credit to surprising lies. There was
indeed necessary a degree of credit, previous to
this delight; and there was necessary a delight,
in order to enforce any degree of credit. But so
it was, that the pleasure rose, in a proportion to
the wonder; and if the love of wonder was but
gratified, no matter whether the tale was founded upon a witch or an Egeria; on a rat, a pi-
geon, the pummel of a sword, a bloated Sibyl,
or a three-foot stool.

Of all writers that bear any resemblance to
these originals, those who approach the nearest
are such as describe their extraordinary dreams
and visions. Of ostentation we may not, perad-
venture, accuse them, who claim to themselves
no other than the merit of spectators. Of want
of abilities we must not censure them; when we

are

are given to know that their imagination had no more part in the affair, than a whited wall has, in thofe various figures which fome crafty artift reprefents thereon.

THE firft meditation of a folitary, is the behaviour of men in active life. Haplefs fpecies, I cried, how very grofsly art thou miftaken! How very fupine, while youth permits thee to gain the prize of virtue by reftraint! how very refolute when thine age leaves nothing to reftrain thee! thou giveft a loofe to thine inclinations, till they lofe their very being; and, like a lamp overwhelmed with oil, are extinguifhed by indulgence. What folly to dream of virtue, when there is no longer roc·i for felf-denial; or, when the enemy expires by ficknefs, to demand the honour of a triumph!——Mufing upon this fubject, I fell into a profound flumber; and the vifion with which it furnifhed me, fhall fupply materials for this effay.

I was, methought, tranfported into a winding valley, on each fide of whofe area, fo far as my eye could fee, were held up (in the manner of a picture) all the pleafing objects either of art or nature. Hills rofe one beyond another, crowned with trees, or adorned with edifices; broken rocks contrafted with lawns, and foaming rivers poured headlong over them; gilded fpires enlivened even the fun-fhine; and lonefome ruins, by the fide of woods, gave a folemnity to the fhade. It would be endlefs, or rather impoffible, to give an idea of the vaft variety. It feemed, as though people of whatever inclinations might here meet with their favourite object.

WHILE I ftood amazed, and even confounded, at fo aftonifhing a landfcape; an old man approached towards me, and offered his affiftance in allevating my furprife. You obferve, fays he, in the middle path, a train of fprightly female pilgrims *, conducted by a matron † of a graver caft. She is habited, as you may obferve, in a robe far more plain and fimple than that of any amidft her followers. It is her province to reftrain her pupils, that the objects glittering on each fide may not feduce them to make excurfions, from which they fcarce ever find their right way again. You may not, perhaps, fufpect the gulfs and precipices that lie intermixed amidft a fcenery fo delightful to the eye. You fee, indeed, at a confiderable diftance, the gilt dome of a temple, raifed on columns of the whiteft marble. I muft inform you, that within this temple refides a lady ‡, weaving wreaths of immortal amaranth for that worthy matron, if fhe exert her authority; and, as their obedience is more or lefs entire, fhe has alfo garlands of inferiour luftre to recompenfe the ladies in her train.

YOUR own fagacity, added he, will fupply the place of farther inftructions, and then vanifhed in an inftant.

THE fpace before me, as it appeared, was croffed by four fucceffive rivers. Over thefe were

* The Paffions.   † Reafon.   ‡ Virtue.

thrown

thrown as many bridges, and beyond each of thefe ftreams the ground feemed to vary its degree of luftre, as much as if it had lain under a different climate. On the fide of each of thefe rivers appeared, as I thought, a receptacle for travellers; fo that the journey feemed to be portioned into four diftinct ftages. It is poffible that thefe were meant to reprefent the periods of a man's life; which may be diftinguifhed by the names of infancy, youth, manhood, and old age.

During the firft ftage, our travellers proceeded without much difturbance. Their excurfions were of no greater extent than to crop a primrofe, or a daify, that grew on the way-fide: and in thefe their governefs indulged them. She gave them but few checks, and they afforded her but little occafion. But when they arrived at the fecond period, the cafe then was greatly altered. The young ladies grew vifibly enamoured of the beauties on each fide; and the governefs began to feel a confcioufnefs of her duty to reftrain them. They petitioned clamoroufly to make one fhort excurfion; and met with a decent refufal. One of them, that vifibly fhewed herfelf the greateft vixen and romp * amongft them, had a thoufand arts and ftratagems to circumvent her well-meaning governefs. I muft here mention, what I remarked afterwards, that fome of the pupils felt greater attractions in one ftage; and fome in another. And the fcene

* Love.

H 2   before

before them being well variegated with moffy banks, and purling ftreams, frifking lambs, and piping fhepherds; infpired a longing that was inexpreffible, to one that feemed of an amorous complexion. She requefted to make a fhort digreffion; pointed to the band of fhepherds dancing; and, as I obferved, prefented a glafs, through which the matron might diftinctly view them. The governefs applied the glafs, and it was wonderful to trace the change it effected. She, who before had with much conftancy oppofed the prayers of her petitioner, now began to lean towards her demands; and, as if fhe herfelf were not quite indifferent to the fcene of pleafure fhe had beheld, grew remifs in her difcipline; foftened the language of diffent; and, with a gentle reprimand, fuffered her pupil to elope. After this, however, fhe winked her eyes; that fhe might not at leaft bear teftimony to the ftep fhe did not approve. When the lady had gratified her curiofity, fhe returned for the prefent; but with an appetite more inflamed, and more impatient to repeat her frolic. The governefs appeared uneafy, and to repent of her own compliance; and reafon good fhe had; confidering the confidence it gave her pupil, and the weight it took from her own authority.

THEY were not paffed far from the fecond ftage of their journey, ere they all determined to rebel, and fubmit to the tyranny of their leader no longer.

ANOTHER now took the lead; and feizing an embroidered handkerchief, completely hood-

winked

winked the directrefs. All now was tumult,
anarchy, difagreement, and confufion. They
led their guide along, blindfold, not without
propofals of downright murder. They foon loft
fight of the regular path, and ftrode along with
amazing rapidity. I fhould, however, except
fome few *, who, being of a complexion naturally languid, and thus deprived of their protect-
refs, had neither conftancy to keep the road,
nor fpirit enough to ftray far from it. Thefe
found the utmoft of their inclination gratified,
in treafuring up fhells from the banks of the ri-
ver, fcooping foffils from the rocks, or prefer-
ving plants that grew in the valley. A moth or
butterfly afforded them a chace, and a grub or
beetle was a fuitable companion. But to return
to the vagabonds.

THE lady that performed the feat of blinding
her governefs, for a time, bore the chief rule;
and held the reft in a ftate of fervitude †. She
feemed to be indeed formed for that power and
grandeur, which was her delight; being of a fta-
ture remarkably tall, with an air of dignity in
her countenance. Not but others would fometimes infift upon fome temporary gratification.
As they fhaped their way to a great city, ‡ one
would loll and loiter on a bed of rofes; another
would join the dance of fhepherds, and fometimes retire with ‖ one into the covert. A ╪ third
would not move a ftep further, till fhe had ga-

* The virtuofo-paffion.   † Ambition.   ‡ Indolence.
‖ Gallantry.   ╪ Avarice.

H 3   thered

thered some ore that was washed from the mountains. When they entered the city, their dissi-
pation was yet more observable. * One intoxi-
cated herself with cordials; † another went in
quest of lace and equipage. The ‡ lady, however, at this time most enterprising, and who
(as I mentioned before) had given such a turn to
their affairs, discovered a strange fondness herself for lawn and ermine, embroidered stars, and
golden collars. However difficult it seemed to
reach them, or how little necessary soever they
seemed to happiness, these alone engaged her attention; and to these alone her hopes aspired.
Nay she went so far, as, in failure of these, to
resolve on misery and wilful wretchedness.

SHE at length succeeded, at least so far, as
to find how little they enhanced her happiness;
and her former compeers having ruined their
constitutions, were once again desirous to have
their queen reign over them. In short, their
loyalty regained the ascendant; insomuch, that
with one consent they removed the bandage from
her eyes, and vowed to obey her future directions.

SHE promised to procure them all the happiness that was consistent with their present state;
and advised them all to follow her towards the
path they had forsaken.

OUR travellers, in a little time after this, passed over the bridge that introduced them to their
closing stage. The subjects, very orderly, re-

* Ebriety.   † Pride and Vanity.   ‡ Ambition.

pentant,

pentant, and demiſſive; the governeſs, more rigid and imperious than ever. The former, wi-
thered, decrepit, languiſhing; the latter, in greater vigour, and more beautiful than before. Time
appeared to produce in her, a very oppoſite effect to that it wrought in her companions. She
ſeemed, indeed, no more that eaſy ductile creature, inſulted and borne away by the whims of
her companions. She appeared more judicious
in the commands ſhe gave, and more rigorous in
the execution. In ſhort, both her own activity,
and the ſupine lethargy of thoſe whom ſhe conducted, united to make way for her unlimited
authority. Now, indeed, a more limited rule
might have ſecured obedience, and maintained
a regularity. The ladies were but little ſtruck
with the glare of objects on each ſide the way.
One alone I muſt except, whom I beheld look
wiſhfully, with a retorted eye, towards the gold-
en ore waſhed down by the torrents. The governeſs repreſented, in the ſtrongeſt terms, that
theſe materials could not be imported into the
realms they were about to enter. That, were
this even the caſe, they could be there of no importance. However ſhe had not extirpated the
bias of this craving dame, when they approached the temple to which I formerly alluded.

THE temple ſtood upon a lofty hill, half en-
circled with trees of never-fading verdure. Between the milk-white columns (which were of
the Doric order, the baſes gilt, as alſo the capi-
tals) a blaze of glory iſſued, of ſuch ſuperiour
luſtre,

luftre, than none befide the governefs was able to approach it. She, indeed, with a dejected countenance, drew near unto the goddefs; who gently waved her hand, in the way of falutation.

THE matron feemed lefs dazzled, than delighted, with her exceffive beauty. She accofted her with reverence, and with much diffidence began to mention their pretenfion to her favour. " She " muft own, fhe had been too remifs in the be- " ginning of her government; fhe hoped it " would be attributed to inexperience in the fub- " tle wiles of her fellow-travellers. She flatter- " ed herfelf, that her feverity towards the con- " clufion of her journey might in fome fort " make atonement for her mifbehaviour in the " beginning. Laftly, that fhe fometimes found " it impoffible to hear the dictates of the god- " defs amid the clamours of her pupils, and the " din of their perfuafions."

To this the goddefs made reply.

" You have heard," faid fhe, " no doubt, that " the favours I beftow, are by no means con- " fiftent with a ftate of inactivity. The only " time when you were allowed an opportunity " to deferve them, was the time when your pu- " pils were the moft refractory and perverfe. " The honours you expect in my court, are pro- " portioned to the difficulty of a good under- " taking. May you, hereafter, partake them, " in reward of your more vigorous conduct: for " the prefent you are little entitled to any recom-

" penfe

" penfe from me. As to your pupils, I obferve,
" they have paffed fentence upon themfelves."

AT this inftant of time the bell rung for fup-
per, and awaked me ; I found the gardener by
my fide, prepared to plant a parcel of trees ;
and that I had flumbered away the hours, in
which I fhould have given him fuitable directions.

U N

UNCONNECTED THOUGHTS
on GARDENING.

GARDENING may be divided into three fpecies——kitchen-gardening—parterre-gar-
dening—and landfcape, or picturefque gardening : which latter is the fubject intended in
the following pages.—It confifts in pleafing the
imagination by fcenes of grandeur, beauty, or
variety. Convenience merely has no fhare here,
any farther than as it pleafes the imagination.

PERHAPS the divifion of the pleafures of imagination, according as they are ftruck by the
great, the various, and the beautiful, may be
accurate enough for my prefent purpofe : why
each of them affects us with pleafure, may be
traced in other authors. See Burke, Hutchin-
fon, Gerard. The theory of agreeable fenfa-
fations, &c. *

THERE feems, however, to be fome objects
which afford a pleafure not reducible to either of
the foregoing heads. A ruin, for inftance, may
be neither new to us, nor majeftic, nor beautiful, yet afford that pleafing melancholy which
proceeds from a reflection on decayed magnificence. For this reafon an able gardener fhould
avail himfelf of objects, perhaps, not very ftri-

---

* GARDEN-SCENES may perhaps be divided into the fublime, the beautiful, and the melancholy or penfive ; to which
laft I know not but we may affign a middle place betwixt the
former two, as being in fome fort compofed of both. See
Burke's fublime, &c,

king,.

king, if they ferve to connect ideas that convey reflections of the pleafing kind.

OBJECTS fhould indeed be lefs calculated to ftrike the immediate eye, than the judgment or well-formed imagination ; as in painting.

IT is no objection to the pleafure of novelty, that it makes an ugly object more difagreeable. It is enough that it produces a fuperiority be-twixt things in other refpects equal. It feems, on fome occafions, to go even further. Are there not broken rocks and rugged grounds, to which we can hardly attribute either beauty or grandeur, and yet when introduced near an ex-tent of lawn, impart a pleafure equal to more fhapely fcenes ? Thus a feries of lawn, though ever fo beautiful, may fatiate and cloy, unlefs the eye paffes to them from wilder fcenes ; and then they acquire the grace of novelty.

VARIETY appears to me to derive good part of its effect from novelty ; as the eye, paffing from one form or colour, to a form or colour of a different kind, finds a degree of novelty in its prefent object which affords immediate fatisfac-tion.

VARIETY however, in fome inftances, may be carried to fuch excefs as to lofe its whole effect. I have obferved ceilings fo crammed with ftucco-ornaments, that, although of the moft different kinds, they have produced an uniformity. A fufficient quantity of undecorated fpace is necef-fary to exhibit fuch decorations to advantage.

GROUND fhould firft be confidered with an eye to its peculiar character : whether it be the grand,

grand, the favage, the fprightly, the melancholy, the horrid, or the beautiful. As one or other of thefe characters prevail, one may fomewhat ftrengthen its effect, by allowing every part fome denomination, and then fupporting its title by fuitable appendages.—For inftance, The lover's walk may have affignation-feats, with proper mottoes—Urns to faithful lovers—Trophies, garlands, &c. by means of art.

WHAT an advantage muft fome Italian feats derive from the circumftance of being fituate on ground mentioned in the claffics ? And, even in England, where-ever a park or garden happens to have been the fcene of any event in hiftory, one would furely avail one's felf of that circumftance, to make it more interefting to the imagination. Mottoes fhould allude to it, columns, &c. record it ; verfes moralize upon it ; and curiofity receive its fhare of pleafure.

IN defigning a houfe and gardens, it is happy when there is an opportunity of maintaining a fubordination of parts; the houfe fo luckily placed as to exhibit a view of the whole defign. I have fometimes thought that there was room for it to refemble an epic or dramatic poem. It is rather to be wifhed than required, that the more ftriking fcenes may fucceed thofe which are lefs fo.

TASTE depends much upon temper. Some prefer Tibullus to Virgil, and Virgil to Homer—Hagley to Perfield, and Perfield to the Welfh mountains. This occafions the different preferences that are given to fituations——A garden
ftrikes

ftrikes us moft, where the grand, and the pleafing fucceed, not intermingle, with each other.

I BELIEVE, however, the fublime has generally a deeper effect than the merely beautiful.

I USE the words *landfcape* and *profpect*, the
former as expreffive of home fcenes, the latter of
diftant images. Profpects fhould take in the blue
diftant hills; but never fo remotely, that they be
not diftinguifhable from clouds. Yet this mere
extent is what the vulgar value.

LANDSCAPE fhould contain variety enough to
form a picture upon canvas; and this is no bad
teft, as I think the landfcape-painter is the gardener's beft defigner. The eye requires a fort of
balance here; but not fo as to encroach upon
probable nature. A wood, or hill, may balance
a houfe or obelifk; for exactnefs would be difpleafing. We form our notions from what we
have feen; and though, could we comprehend the
univerfe, we might perhaps find it uniformly regular; yet the portions that we fee of it habi-
tuate our fancy to the contrary.

THE eye fhould always look rather down upon
water: cuftomary nature makes this requifite.
I know nothing more fenfibly difpleafing than
Mr T——'s flat ground betwixt his terras and
his water.

IT is not eafy to account for the fondnefs of
former times for ftrait-lined avenues to their
houfes; ftrait-lined walks through their woods;
and, in fhort, every kind of ftrait line; where
the foot is to travel over, what the eye has done
before. This circumftance is one objection. An-

other, fomewhat of the fame kind, is the repetition of the fame object, tree after tree, for
a length of way together. A third is, that this
identity is purchafed by the lofs of that variety
which the natural country fupplies every where,
in a greater or lefs degree. To ftand ftill and
furvey fuch avenues, may afford fome flender
fatisfaction, through the change derived from
perfpective; but to move on continually, and find
no change of fcene in the leaft attendant on our
change of place, muft give actual pain to a perfon of tafte. For fuch an one to be condemned
to pafs along the famous vifta from * Mofcow
to Peterfburg, or that other from Agra to Lahor
in India, muft be as difagreeable a fentence, as to
be condemned to labour at the galleys. I conceived fome idea of the fenfation he muft feel,
from walking but a few minutes immured betwixt
Lord D——'s high-fhorn yew-hedges, which
run exactly parallel, at the diftance of about ten
feet, and are contrived perfectly to exclude all
kind of objects whatfoever.

WHEN a building, or other object, has been
once viewed from its proper point, the foot fhould
never travel to it by the fame path which the
eye has travelled over before. Lofe the object,
and draw nigh, obliquely.

THE fide-trees in viftas fhould be fo circum-
ftanced as to afford a probability that they grew
by nature.

RUINATED ftructures appear to derive their
power of pleafing from the irregularity of fur-

* In Montefquieu, on T. &c.

face,

face, which is VARIETY; and the latitude they afford the imagination to conceive an enlargement of their dimenfions, or to recollect any events or circumftances appertaining to their priftine grandeur, fo far as concerns grandeur and folemnity. The breaks in them fhould be as bold and abrupt as poffible.—If mere beauty be aimed at (which however is not their chief excellence), the waving line, with more eafy tranfitions, will become of greater importance.—Events relating to them may be fimulated by numberlefs little artifices; but it is ever to be remembered, that high hills and fudden defcents are moft fuitable to caftles; and fertile vales, near wood and water, moft imitative of the ufual fituation for abbeys and religious houfes; large oaks, in particular, are effential to thefe latter,

Whofe branching arms, and reverend height
Admit a dim religious light.

A cottage is a pleafing object, partly on account of the variety it may introduce; on account of the tranquillity that feems to reign there; and perhaps, (I am fomewhat afraid), on account of the pride of human nature.

Longe alterius fpeÉlare laborem.

In a fcene prefented to the eye, objects fhould never lie fo much to the right or left as to give it any uneafinefs in the examination. Sometimes, however, it may be better to admit valuable objects even with this difadvantage. They fhould elfe never be feen beyond a certain angle. The eye muft be eafy before it can be pleafed.

No

No mere slope from one side to the other can be agreeable ground : The eye requires a balance — *i. e.* a degree of uniformity : but this may be otherwise effected, and the rule should be understood with some limitation.

— Each alley has its brother,
And half the plat-form just reflects the other.

LET us examine what may be said in favour of that regularity which Mr Pope exposes. Might he not seemingly as well object to the difposition of an human face, because it has an eye or cheek that is the very picture of its companion ? Or does not Providence, who has obferved this regularity in the external ftructure of our bodies, and difregarded it within, feem to confider it as a beauty? The arms, the limbs, and the feveral parts of them correfpond ; but it is not the fame cafe with the thorax and the abdomen. I believe one is generally folicitous for a kind of balance in a landfcape, and, if I am not miftaken, the painters generally furnifh one : A building for inftance on one fide, contrafted by a group of trees, a large oak, or a rifing hill on the other. Whence then does this tafte proceed, but from the love we bear to regularity in perfection? After all, in regard to gardens, the fhape of ground, the difpofition of trees, and the figure of water, muft be facred to nature ; and no forms muft be allowed that make a difcovery of art.

ALL trees have a character analogous to that of men : Oaks are in all refpects the perfect image

ruage of the manly character: In former times
I fhould have faid, and in prefent times I think
I am authorifed to fay, the Britifh one. As a
brave man is not fuddenly either elated by pro-
fperity, or depreffed by adverfity, fo the oak difplays not its verdure on the fun's firft approach,
nor drops it on his firft departure. Add to this
its majeftic appearance, the rough grandeur of its
bark, and the wide protection of its branches.

A LARGE, branching, aged oak, is perhaps
the moft venerable of all inanimate objects.

URNS are more folemn, if large and plain;
more beautiful, if lefs and ornamented. So-
lemnity is perhaps their point, and the fituation
of them fhould ftill co-operate with it.

By the way, I wonder that lead ftatues are
not more in vogue in our modern gardens.
Though they may not exprefs the finer lines of
an human body, yet they feem perfectly well calculated, on account of their duration, to embel-
lifh landfcapes, were they fome degrees inferiour
to what we generally behold. A ftatue in a
room challenges examination, and is to be examined critically 'as a ftatue. A ftatue in a
garden is to be confidered as one part of a fcene
or landfcape; the minuter touches are no more
effential to it, than a good landfcape-painter
would efteem them were he to reprefent a ftatue
in his picture.

APPARENT art, in its proper province, is almoft as important as apparent nature. They
contraft agreeably; but their provinces ever
fhould be kept diftinct.

WHERE

WHERE fome artificial beauties are fo dexte-
roufly managed that one cannot but conceive them
natural, fome natural ones are fo extremely fortunate that one is ready to fwear they are artificial.

CONCERNING fcenes, the more uncommon
th·y appear, the better, provided they form a
picture, and include nothing that pretends to be
of nature's production, and is not. The fhape
of ground, the fite of trees, and the fall of water, nature's province. Whatever thwarts her
is treafon.

On the other hand, buildings and the works
of art, need have no other reference to nature
than that they afford the *ευσμενον* with which the
human mind is delighted.

ART fhould never be allowed to fet a foot in
the province of nature, otherwife than clandeftinely and by night. Whenever fhe is allowed
to appear here, and men begin to compromife
the difference;—night, Gothicifm, confufion, and
abfolute chaos are come again.

To fee one's urns, obelifks, and waterfalls
hid open ; the nakednefs of our beloved miftreffes, the naiads, and the dryads, expofed by
that ruffian winter to univerfal obfervation ; is a
feverity fcarcely to be fupported by the help of
blazing hearths, cheerful companions, and a
bottle of the moft grateful burgundy.

THE works of a perfon that builds, begin immediately to decay ; while thofe of him who
plants begin directly to improve. In this, planting promifes a more lafting pleafure, than building ; which, were it to remain in equal perfection,

tion, would at beft begin to moulder and want
repairs in imagination. Now trees have a circumftance that fuits our tafte, and that is annual
variety. It is inconvenient indeed, if they caufe
our love of life to take root and flourifh with
them; whereas the very famenefs of our ftructures will, without the help of dilapidation,
ferve to wean us from our attachment to them.

IT is a cuftom in fome countries to condemn
the characters of thofe (after death) that have
neither planted a tree, nor begat a child.

THE tafte of the citizen and of the mere peafant are in all refpects the fame. The former
gilds his balls; paints his ftonework and ftatues.
white; plants his trees in lines or circles; cuts
his yew-trees four-fquare or conic; or gives
them, what he can, of the refemblance of birds,
or bears, or men; fquirts up his rivulet in jet-
teaus; in fhort, admires no part of nature, but
her ductility; exhibits every thing that is gla-
ring, that implies expenfe, or that effects a furprife becaufe it is unnatural. The peafant is his
admirer.

IT is always to be remembered in gardening,
that fublimity or magnificence, and beauty or
variety, are very different things. Every fcene
we fee in nature is either tame and infipid, or
compounded of thofe. It often happens that
the fame ground may receive from art, either
certain degrees of fublimity and magnificence, or
certain degrees of variety and beauty, or a mixture of each kind. In this cafe it remains to be
confidered in which light they can be rendered
                                                    moft

moſt remarkable, whether as objects of beauty,. or magnificence.. Even the temper of the proprietor ſhould not perhaps. be wholly diſregarded : for certain complexions of ſoul will prefer an orange tree or a myrtle to an oak or.cedar.. However, this. ſhould not induce a gardener to. parcel.out a lawn into knots of ſhrubbery, or inveſt a mountain with. a garb of roſes. This. would be like dreſſing a giant in a ſarſenet gown, or a Saracen's head in a Bruſſels night-cap. Indeed the ſmall and circular clumps of firs, which. I ſee planted upon ſome. fine large ſwells, put 'me often in mind of a. coronet placed on an elephant or camel's back.. I ſay a. gardener ſhould. not do this, any more than a poet ſhould. attempt to write of the king of. Pruſſia in the ſtyle of Philips. On the other. ſide, what would. become. of Leſbia's ſparrow ſhould it. be treated in the ſame language with the anger of Achilles ?

G ARDENERS may be divided into three ſorts, the landſcape-gardener,. the parterre-gardener, and the kitchen-gardener, agreeably to our firſt diviſion of gardens.

I. HAVE uſed the word *landſcape-gardeners;* becauſe, in purſuance of our preſent taſte in gardening, every good. painter of landſcape appears to me the.moſt proper deſigner. The misfortune of it is, that. theſe painters are apt to regard the execution of their work, much more than the choice of ſubject..

THE art of diſtancing and. approximating, comes truly within their ſphere : the former by the gradual diminution of diſtinctneſs, and of

fize ;

size ; the latter by the reverse. A strait-lined avenue that is widened in front, and planted there with yew-trees, then firs, then with trees more and more fady, till they end in the almond-willow, or silver osier ; will produce a very remarkable deception of the former kind ; which deception will be increased, if the nearer dark trees are proportionable, and truly larger than those at the end of the avenue that are more fady.

· To distance a building, plant as near as you can to it, two or three circles of different coloured greens. — Evergreens are best for all such purposes. Suppose the outer one of holly, and the next of laurel, &c. The consequence will be, that the imagination immediately allows a space betwixt these circles and another betwixt the house and them ; and as the imagined space is indeterminate, if your building be dim-coloured, it will not appear inconsiderable. The imagination is a greater magnifier than a microscopic glass. And on this head, I have known some instances, where, by shewing intermediate ground, the distance has appeared less, than while an hedge or grove concealed it.

HEDGES, appearing as such, are universally bad. They discover art in nature's province.

TREES in hedges partake of their artificiality, and become a part of them. There is no more sudden, and obvious improvement, than an hedge removed, and the trees remaining ; yet not in such manner as to mark out the former hedge.

WATER

WATER fhould ever appear, as an irregular lake, or winding ftream.

ISLANDS give beauty, if the water be adequate; but leffen grandeur through variety.

IT was the wife remark of fome fagacious obferver, that familiarity is for the moft part productive of contempt. Gracelefs offspring of fo amiable a parent! Unfortunate beings that we are, whofe enjoyments muft be either checked, or prove deftructive of themfelves. Our paffions are permitted to fip a little pleafure; but are extinguifhed by indulgence, like a lamp overwhelmed with oil. Hence we neglect the beauty with which we have been intimate; nor would any addition it could receive, prove an equivalent for the advantage it derived from the firft impreffion. Thus negligent of graces that have the merit of reality, we too often prefer imaginary ones that have only the charm of novelty: And hence we may account, in general, for the preference of art to nature, in our old-fafhioned gardens.

ART, indeed, is often requifite to collect and epitomize the beauties of nature; but fhould never be fuffered to fet her mark upon them: I mean in regard to thofe articles that are of nature's province; the fhaping of ground, the planting of trees, and the difpofition of lakes and rivulets. Many more particulars will foon occur, which, however, fhe is allowed to regulate, fomewhat clandeftinely, upon the following account.—Man is not capable of comprehending the univerfe at one furvey. Had he faculties equal to this, he might well be cenfured for any minute

nute regulations of his own. It were the fame, as if, in his prefent fituation, he ftrove to find amufement in contriving the fabric of an ant's neft, or the partitions of a bee-hive. But we are placed in the corner of a fphere ; endued neither with organs, nor allowed a ftation proper to give us an univerfal view ; or to exhibit to us the variety, the orderly proportions, and difpofitions of the fyftem. We perceive many breaks and blemifhes, feveral neglected and unvariegated places in the part ; which, in the whole, would appear either imperceptible, or beautiful. And we might as rationally expect a fnail to be fatisfied with the beauty of our parterres, flopes, and terraffes — or an ant to prefer our buildings to her own orderly range of granaries, as that man fhould be fatisfied, without a fingle thought that he can improve the fpot that falls to his fhare. But, though art be neceffary for collecting nature's beauties, by what reafon is fhe authorifed to thwart and to oppofe her ? Why fantaftically endeavour to humanize thofe vegetables, of which nature, difcreet nature, thought it proper to make trees ? Why endow the vegetable bird with wings, which nature has made momentarily dependent upon the foil ? Here art feems very affectedly to make a difplay of that induftry, which it is her glory to conceal. The ftone which reprefents an afterifk, is valued only on account of its natural production : Nor do we view with pleafure the laboured carvings and futile diligence of Gothic artifts. We view with much more fatisfaction fome plain Grecian fabric,

fabric, where art, indeed, has been equally, but lefs vifibly, induftrious.   It is thus we, indeed, admire the fhining texture of the filk-worm; but we loath the puny author, when fhe thinks proper to emerge ; and to difguft us with the appearance of fo vile a grub.

BU T this is merely true in regard to the particulars of nature's province ; wherein art can only appear as the moft abject vaffal, and had, therefore, better not appear at all.   The cafe is different where fhe. has the direction of buildings, ufeful or ornamental ; or, perhaps, claims as much honour from temples, as the deities to whom they are infcribed.   Here then it is her intereft to be feen as much as poffible :`and, though nature appear doubly beautiful by the contraft her ftructures furnifh, it is not eafy for her to confer a benefit which nature, on her fide, will not repay.

A RURAL fcene to me is never perfect without the addition of fome kind of building : Indeed I have known a fcar of rock-work, in great meafure, fupply the deficiency.

IN gardening it is no fmall point to enforce either grandeur. or beauty by furprife ; for inftance, by abrupt tranfition from their contraries, —but to lay a ftrefs upon furprife only ; for example, on the furprife occafioned by an aha ! without including any nobler purpofe ; is a fymptom of bad tafte, and a violent fondnefs for mere concetto.

GRANDEUR and beauty are fo very oppofite, that you often diminifh the one as you increafe
the

the other. Variety is moſt akin to the latter, ſimplicity to the former.

SUPPOSE a large hill, varied by art, with large patches of different-coloured clumps, ſcars of rock, chalk-quarries, villages, or farm-houſes ; you will have, perhaps, a more beautiful ſcene, but much leſs grand than it was before.

IN many inſtances, it is moſt eligible to compound your ſcene of beauty and grandeur.—Suppoſe a magnificent ſwell ariſing out of a well-variegated valley ; it would be diſadvantageous to increaſe its beauty, by means deſtructive to its magnificence.

THERE may poſſibly, but there ſeldom happens, any occaſion to fill up valleys, with trees or otherwiſe. It is for the moſt part the gardener's buſineſs to remove trees, or ought that fills up the low ground ; and to give, as far as nature allows, an artificial eminence to the high.

THE hedge-row apple-trees in Herefordſhire afford a moſt beautiful ſcenery, at the time they are in bloſſom : but the proſpect would be really grander, did it conſiſt of ſimple foliage. For the ſame reaſon, a large oak (or beech) in autumn is a grander object than the ſame in ſpring. The ſprightly green is then obfuſcated.

SMOOTHNESS and eaſy tranſitions are no ſmall ingredients in the beautiful ; abrupt and rectangular breaks have more of the nature of the ſublime. Thus a tapering ſpire is, perhaps, a more beautiful object than a tower, which is grander.

MANY of the different opinions relating to

the

the preference to be given to feats, villas, &c. are owing to want of diftinction betwixt the beautiful and the magnificent. Both the former and the latter pleafe; but there are imaginations particularly adapted to the one, and to the o-ther.

Mr Addison thought an open uninclofed champaign country formed the beft landfcape. Somewhat here is to be confidered. Large, unva-riegated, fimple objects have the beft pretenfions to fublimity; a large mountain, whofe fides are unvaried with objects, is grander than one with infinite variety; but then its beauty is proportion-ably lefs.

However, I think a plain fpace near the eye gives it a kind of liberty it loves; and then the picture, whether you chufe the grand or beautiful, fhould be held up at its proper di-ftance. Variety is the principal ingredient in beauty, and fimplicity is effential to grandeur.

Offensive objects at a proper diftance, ac-quire even a degree of beauty; for inftance, ftubble, fallow ground —

On

On POLITICS.

PERHAPS men of the moſt different ſects and parties very frequently think the ſame ; only vary in their phraſe and language. At leaſt, if one examines their firſt principles, which very often coincide, it were a point of prudence, as well as candour, to conſider the reſt as nothing more.

A COURTIER's dependent is a beggar's dog.

IF national reflections are unjuſt, becauſe there are good men in all nations, are not national wars upon much the ſame footing ?

A GOVERNMENT is inexcuſable for employing fooliſh miniſters ; becauſe they may examine a man's head, though they cannot his heart.

I FANCY the proper means of increaſing the love we bear our native country, is to reſide ſome time in a foreign one.

THE love of popularity ſeems little elſe than the love of being beloved ; and is only blameable when a perſon aims at the affections of a people by means in appearance honeſt, but in their end pernicious and deſtructive.

THERE ought, no doubt, to be heroes in ſociety as well as butchers ; and who knows but the neceſſity of butchers (inflaming and ſtimulating the paſſions with animal food) might at firſt occaſion the neceſſity of heroes ? Butchers, I believe, were prior.

THE whole myſtery of a courtly behaviour

ſeems

feems included in the power of making general favours appear particular ones.

A MAN of remarkable genius may afford to pafs by a piece of wit, if it happen to border on abufe. A little genius is obliged to catch at every witticifm indifcriminately.

INDOLENCE is a kind of centripetal force.

IT feems idle to rail at ambition, merely becaufe it is a boundlefs paffion ; or rather is not this circumftance an argument in its favour ? If one would be employed or amufed through life, fhould we not make choice of a paffion that will keep one long in play ?

A SPORTSMAN of vivacity will make choice of that game which will prolong his diverfion : A fox that will fupport the chace till night, is better game than a rabbit that will not afford him half an hour's entertainment. E.

THE fubmiffion of Prince Hal to the civil magiftrate that committed him, was more to his honour than all the conquefts of Henry the Fifth in France.

THE moft animated focial pleafure that I can conceive, may be, perhaps, felt by a general after a fuccefsful engagement, or in it ; I mean by fuch commanders as have fouls equal to their occupation. This, however, feems paradoxical, and requires fome explanation.

RESISTANCE to the reigning powers is juftifiable, upon a conviction that their government is inconfiftent with the good of the fubject ; that our interpofition tends to eftablifh better meafures, and this without a probability of occafion-

ing

ing evils that may overbalance them. But thefe confiderations muft never be feparated.

PEOPLE are, perhaps, more vitious in towns, becaufe they have fewer natural objeéts there to employ their attention — or admiration ; like-wife becaufe one vitious charaéter tends to en-courage and keep another in countenance. How-ever it be, excluding accidental circumftances, I believe the largeft cities are the moft vitious of all others.

LAWS are generally found to be nets of fuch a texture, as the little creep through, the great break through, and the middle-fized are alone entangled in.

THOUGH I have no fort of inclination to vin-dicate the late rebellion, yet I am led by candour to make fome diftinéction between the immorality of its abettors, and the illegality of their offence. My Lord Hardwicke, in his condemnation-fpeech, remarks, with great propriety, that the laws of all nations have adjudged rebellion to be the worft of crimes. And in regard to civil focieties, I believe there is none but madmen will difpute it. But furely, with regard to confcience, erro-neous judgments and ill-grounded convictions may render it fome people's duty. Sin does not confift in any deviation from received opinion ; it does not depend upon the underftanding, but the will. Now, if it appear that a man's opi-nion has happened to mifplace his duty, and this opinion has not been owing to any vitious defire of indulging his appetites ; — in fhort, if his own reafon, liable to err, have biaffed his will,

K 3

ther

rather than his will any way contributed to biafs and deprave his reafon, he will, perhaps, appear guilty before none, befide an earthly tribunal.

A PERSON's right to refift depends upon a conviction, that the government is ill managed ; that others have more claim to manage it, or will adminifter it better ; that he, by his re-fiftance, can introduce a change to its advantage, and this without any confequential evils that will bear proportion to the faid advantage.

WHETHER this were not in appearance the cafe of Balmerino, I will not prefume to fay ; how conceived, or from what delufion fprung. But as, I think, he was reputed an honeft man in other refpects, one may guefs his behaviour was rather owing to the mifreprefentations of his reafon, than to any depravity, perverfenefs, or difingenuity of his will.

IF a perfon ought heartily to ftickle for any caufe, it fhould be that of moderation. Mode-raion fhould be his party.

EGOTISMS,

EGOTISMS,

FROM MY OWN SENSATIONS.

I.

I HATE maritime expreffions, fimiles, and allu-fions ; my diflike, I fuppofe, proceeds from the unnaturalnefs of fhipping, and the great fhare which art ever claims in that practice.

II.

I AM thankful that my name is obnoxious to, no pun.

III.

MAY I always have an heart fuperiour, with, oeconomy fuitable, to my fortune.

IV.

INANIMATES, toys, utenfils, feem to merit a kind of affection from us, when they have been our companions through various viciffitudes. I have often viewed my watch, ftandifh, fnuff-box, with this kind of tender regard ; allotting them a degree of friendfhip, which there are fome men who do not deferve..

'Midft many faithlefs only faithful found!

V.

I LOVED Mr Somerville, becaufe he knew fo perfectly what belonged to the flocci-nauci-nihili-pili-fication of money.

VI.

IT is with me in regard to the earth itfelf, as it is in regard to thofe that walk upon its furface..

I

I love to pafs by crouds, and to catch diftant views of the country as I walk along; but I infenfibly chufe to fit where I cannot fee two yards before me.

VII.

I begin, too foon in life, to flight the world more than is confiftent with making a figure in it. The *non eft tanti* of Ovid grows upon me fo faft, that in a few years I fhall have no paffion.

VIII.

I am obliged to the perfon that fpeaks me fair to my face.   I am only more obliged to the man who fpeaks well of me in my abfence alfo. Should I be afked whether I chofe to have a perfon fpeak well of me when abfent or prefent ? I fhould anfwer, the latter ; for were all men to do fo, the former would be infignificant.

IX.

I feel an avarice of focial pleafure, which produces only mortification.   I never fee a town or city in a map, but I figure to myfelf many agreeable perfons in it, with whom I could wifh to be acquainted.

X.

It is a miferable thing to be fenfible of the value of one's time, and yet reftrained by circumftances from making a proper ufe of it.   One feels one's felf fomewhat in the fituation of Admiral Hofier.

XI.

It is a miferable thing to love where one hates ; and yet it is not inconfiftent.

XII.

XII.

THE modern world confiders it as a part of politeneſs, to drop the mention of kindred in all addreſſes to relations. There is no doubt, that it puts our approbation and eſteem upon a leſs partial footing. I think, where I value a friend, I would not ſuffer my relation to be obliterated, even to the twentieth generation. It ſerves to conne&t us cloſer : where-ever I difeſteemed, I would abdicate my firſt couſin.

CIRCUMLOCUTORY, philoſophical obſcenity appears to me the moſt nauſeous of all ſtuff. Shall I ſay it takes away the ſpirit from it, and leaves you nothing but a *caput mortuum;* or ſhall I ſay rather it is a fir---e in an envelope of fine gilt paper, which only raiſes expe&tation ? Could any be allowed to talk obſcenely with a grace, it were downright country-fellows, who uſe an un-affe&ted language : but even among theſe, as they grow old, it partakes again of affe&tation.

IT is ſome loſs of liberty to reſolve on ſchemes beforehand.

THERE are a ſort of people to whom one would allot good wiſhes and perform good offices ; but they are ſometimes thoſe with whom one would by no means ſhare one's time.

I WOULD have all men elevated to as great an height, as they can diſcover a luſtre to the naked eye.

I AM ſurely more inclined (of the two) to pretend a falſe diſdain, than an unreal eſteem.

YET why repine ? I have ſeen manſions on the verge of Wales that convert my farm-houſe

into

into an Hampton-court, and where they fpeak
of a glazed window as a great piece of magnificence. All things figure by comparifon.

I do not fo much want to avoid being cheated, as to afford the expenfe of being fo ; the
generality of mankind being feldom in good humour but whilft they are impofing upon you in
fome fhape or other.

I cannot avoid comparing the eafe and freedom I enjoy, to the cafe of an old fhoe, where
a certain degree of fhabbinefs is joined with the
convenience.

Not Hebrew, Arabic, Syriac, Coptic, nor
even the Chinefe language, feems half fo difficult
to me as the language of refufal.

I actually dreamed that fomebody told me
I muft not print my pieces feparate ; that certain ftars would, if fingle, be hardly confpicuous,
which united in a narrow compafs form a very
fplendid conftellation.

The ways of ballad-fingers, and the cries of
halfpenny-pamphlets, appeared fo extremely humorous, from my lodgings in F —— ftreet, that
it gave me pain to obferve them without a companion to partake. For, alas, laughter is by no
means a folitary entertainment.

Had I a fortune of 8 or 10,000 l. a-year, I
would methinks make myfelf a neighbourhood.
I would firft build a village with a church, and
people it with inhabitants of fome branch of
trade that was fuitable to the country round. I
would then at proper diftances erect a number of
genteel boxes of about 1000 l. a-piece, and amufe
                                    myfelf

myfelf with giving them all the advantages they could receive from tafte. Thefe would I people with a felect number of well-chofen friends, affigning to each annually the fum of 200 l. for life. The falary fhould be irrevocable, in order to give them independency ; the houfe, of a more precarious tenure, that, in cafes of ingratitude, I might introduce another inhabitant.

How plaufible foever this may appear in fpeculation, perhaps a very natural and lively novel might be founded upon the inconvenient confequences of it, when put in execution.

I THINK I have obferved univerfally, that the quarrels of friends in the latter part of life are never truly reconciled. *Male farta gratia nequicquam coit, et refcinditur.* A wound in the friendfhip of young perfons, as in the bark of young trees, may be fo grown over as to leave no fcar. The cafe is very different in regard to old perfons, and old timber. The reafon of this may be accountable from the decline of the focial paffions, and the prevalence of fpleen, fufpicion, and rancour, towards the latter part of life.

THERE is nothing, to me, more irkfome than to hear weak and fervile people repeat with admiration every filly fpeech that falls from a mere perfon of rank and fortune. It is *crambe bis coëta.*——The nonfenfe grows more naufeous through the medium of their admiration, and fhews the venality of vulgar tempers, which can confider fortune as the goddefs of wit.

WHAT pleafure it is to pay one's debts ! I remember to have heard Sir T. Lyttelton make

the

the fame obfervation. It feems to flow from a combination of circumftances, each of which is productive of pleafure. In the firft place, it removes that uneafinefs which a true fpirit feels from dependence and obligation. It affords pleafure to the creditor, and therefore gratifies our focial affection. It promotes that future confidence, which is fo very interefting to an honeft mind : it opens a profpect of being readily fupplied with what we want on future occafions : it leaves a confcioufnefs of our own virtue : and it is a meafure we know to be right, both in point of juftice and of found œconomy. Finally, it is a main fupport of fimple reputation.

IT is a maxim with me, (and I would recommend it to others alfo, upon the fcore of prudence), whenever I lofe a perfon's friendfhip, who generally commences enemy, to engage a frefh friend in his place. And this may be beft effected by bringing over fome of one's enemies ; by which means one is a gainer, having an enemy the lefs, and the fame number of friends. Such a method of proceeding fhould, I think, be as regularly obferved, as the diftribution of vacant ribbons, upon the death of knights of the Garter.

IT has been a maxim with me, to admit of an eafy reconciliation with a perfon whofe offence proceeded from no depravity of heart : but where I was convinced it did fo, to forego, for my own fake, all opportunities of revenge ; to forget the perfons of my enemies as much as I was able, and to call to remembrance, in their

place,

place, the more pleafing idea of my friends. I
am convinced, that I have derived no fmall fhare
of happinefs from this principle.

I HAVE been formerly fo filly as to hope, that
every fervant I had might be made a friend : I
am now convinced, that the nature of fervitude
generally bears a contrary tendency. People's
characters are to be chiefly collected from their
education and place in life : birth itfelf does
but little. Kings in general are born with the
fame propenfities as other men ; but yet it is probable, from the licence and flattery that attends
their education, that they will be more haughty,
more luxurious, and more fubjected to their
paffions, than any men befide. I queftion not
but there are many attorneys born with open and
honeft hearts ; but I know not one that has had
the leaft practice, who is not felfifh, trickifh, and
difingenuous. So it is the nature of fervitude
to difcard all generous motives of obedience,
and to point out no other than thofe fcoundrel
ones of intereft and fear. There are however
fome exceptions to this rule, which I know by
my own experience.

I.

DRESS, like writing, should never appear the effect of too much study and application. On this account, I have seen parts of dress in themselves extremely beautiful, which at the same time subject the wearer to the character of foppishness and affectation.

II.

A MAN's dress in the former part of life should rather tend to set off his person, than to express riches, rank, or dignity; in the latter, the reverse.

III.

EXTREME elegance in liveries, I mean such as is expressed by the more languid colours, is altogether absurd. They ought to be rather gaudy than genteel; if for no other reason, yet for this, that elegance may more strongly distinguish the appearance of the gentleman.

IV.

IT is a point out of doubt with me, that the ladies are most properly the judges of the mens dress, and the men of that of the ladies.

V.

I THINK till thirty, or with some a little longer, people should dress in a way that is most likely to procure the love of the opposite sex.

VI.

THERE are many modes of dress which the
world

world efteems handfome, which are by no means, calculated to fhew the human figure to advantage.

VII.

LOVE can be founded upon nature only, or the appearance of it.—For this reafon, however a peruke may tend to foften the human features, it can very feldom make amends for the mixture of artifice which it difcovers.

VIII.

A RICH drefs adds but little to the beauty of a perfon. It may poffibly create a deference, but that is rather an enemy to love.

Non bene conveniunt, nec in una fede morantur Majeftas et amor. OVID.

IX.

SIMPLICITY can fcarce be carried too far, provided it be not fo fingular as to excite a degree of ridicule. The fame caution may be requifite in regard to the value of your drefs; though fplendour be not neceffary, you muft remove all appearance of poverty, the ladies being rarely enough fagacious to acknowledge beauty through the difguife of poverty. Indeed, I believe fometimes they miftake grandeur of drefs for beauty of perfon.

X.

A PERSON's manner is never eafy, while he feels a confcioufnefs that he is fine. The country-fellow confidered in fome lights appears genteel; but it is not when he is dreffed on Sundays with a large nofegay in his bofom. It is when

L 2   he

he is reaping, making hay, or when he is hedging in his hurden frock. It is then he acts with eafe, and thinks himfelf equal to his apparel.

XI.

WHEN a man has run all lengths himfelf with regard to drefs, there is but one means remaining which can add to his appearance. And this confifts in having recourfe to the utmoft plainnefs in his own apparel, and at the fame time richly garnifhing his footman or horfe. Let the fervant appear as fine as ever you pleafe, the world muft always confider the mafter as his fupcriour. And this is that peculiar excellence fo much admired in the beft painters as well as poets, Raphael as well as Virgil; where fomewhat is left to be fupplied by the fpectator's and reader's imagination.

XII.

METHINKS apparel fhould be rich in the fame proportion as it is gay : it otherwife carries the appearance of fomewhat unfubftantial ; in other words, of a greater defire than ability to make a figure.

XIII.

PERSONS are oftentimes mifled in regard to their choice of drefs, by attending to the beauty of colours, rather than felecting fuch colours as may increafe their own beauty.

XIV.

· I CANNOT fee why a perfon fhould be eftcemed haughty, on account of his tafte for fine cloaths, any more than one who difcovers a fond-

nefs

nefs for birds, flowers, moths, or butterflies. Imagination influences both to feek amufement in glowing colours, only the former endeavours to give them a nearer relation to himfelf. It appears to me, that a perfon may love fplendour without any degree of pride ; which is never connected with this tafte, but when a perfon demands homage on account of the finery he exhibits. Then it ceafes to be tafte, and commences mere ambition. Yet the world is not enough candid to make this effential diftinction.

XV.

The firft inftance an officer gives you of his courage, confifts in wearing cloaths infinitely fuperiour to his rank.

XVI.

Men of quality never appear more amiable than when their drefs is plain. Their birth, rank, title, and its appendages, are at beft invidious ; and as they do not need the affiftance of drefs, fo, by their difclaiming the advantage of it, they make their fuperiority fit more eafy. It is otherwife with fuch as depend alone on perfonal merit ; and it was from hence, I prefume, that Quin afferted he could not afford to go plain.

XVII.

There are certain fhapes and phyfiognomies of fo entirely vulgar a caft, that they could fcarce win refpect even in the country, though they were embellifhed with a drefs as tawdry as a pulpit-cloth.

XVIII. A

XVIII.

A LARGE retinue upon a fmall income, like a large cafcade upon a fmall ftream, tends to dif-cover its tenuity.

XIX.

WHY are perfumes fo much decried? when a perfon, on his approach, diffufes them, does he not revive the idea which the ancients ever entertained concerning the defcent of fuperiour beings, " veiled in a cloud of fragrance ? "

THE loweft people are generally the firft to find fault with fhew or equipage, efpecially that of a perfon lately emerged from his obfcurity. They never once confider that he is breaking the ice for themfelves.

On

On WRITING and BOOKS.

I.

FINE writing is generally the effect of spontaneous thoughts, and a laboured ftyle.

II.

LONG fentences in a fhort compofition, are like large rooms in a little houfe.

III.

THE world may be divided into people that read, people that write, people that think, and fox-hunters.

IV.

INSTEAD of whining complaints concerning the imagined cruelty of their miftreffes, if poets would addrefs the fame to their mufe, they would act more agreeably to nature and to truth.

V.

SUPERFICIAL writers, like the mole, often fancy themfelves deep, when they are exceeding near the furface.

VI.

Sumite materiam veftris, qui fcribitis, aequam.
Viribus ——

AUTHORS often fail by printing their works on a demi-royal, that fhould have appeared on ballad-paper, to make their performance appear laudable.

VII.

THERE is no word in the Latin language, that
signifies

fignifies a female friend. *Amica* means a miftrefs ; and perhaps there is no friendfhip betwixt the fexes wholly difunited from a degree of
love.

VIII.

THE chief advantage that ancient writers can
boaft over modern ones, feems owing to fimplicity. Every noble truth and fentiment was expreffed by the former in the natural manner ; in
word and phrafe, fimple, perfpicuous, and incapable of improvement. What then remained
for later writers but affectation, witticifm, and
conceit ?

IX.

ONE can, now and then, reach an author's
head when he ftoops, and, induced by this circumftance, afpire to meafure height with him.

X.

THE national opinion of a book or treatife is
not always right.—*Eft ubi peccat*—Milton's para-
dife loft is one inftance ; I mean the cold re-
ception it met with at firft.

XI.

PERHAPS an acquaintance with men of genius is rather reputable than fatisfactory. It is as
accountable, as it is certain, that fancy heightens
fenfibility ; fenfibility ftrengthens paffion ; and
paffion makes people humourifts.

YET a perfon of genius is often expected to
fhew more difcretion than another man, and
this on account of that very vivacity which is
his greateft impediment. This happens for want
of

of diftinguifhing betwixt the fanciful talents, and
the dry mathematical operations of the judgment, each of which indifcriminately give the
denomination of a man of genius.

XII.

An actor never gained a reputation by acting
a bad play, nor a mufician by playing on a bad
inftrument.

XIII.

Poets feem to have fame in lieu of moft
temporal advantages. They are too little formed for bufinefs, to be refpected ; too often fear-
ed or envied, to be beloved.

XIV.

Tully ever feemed an inftance to me, how
far a man devoid of courage may be a fpirited
writer.

XV.

One would rather be a ftump of laurel than
the ftump of a church-yard yew-tree.

XVI.

Degere more terrae. Virg.   Vanbrugh feems
to have had this of Virgil in his eye, when he
introduces Mifs Hoyden envying the liberty of a
grey-hound bitch.

XVII.

There is a certain flimzinefs of poetry which
feems expedient in a fong.

XVIII.

Dido, as well as Defdemona *, feems to have

* Lord Shaftefbury.

been

been a mighty admirer of ftrange achievements.

Heu quibus ille,
Jactatus totis, quae bella exhaufta canebat,
Si mihi non, &c.

This may fhew that Virgil, Shakefpear, and Shaftefbury agreed in the fame opinion.

XIX.

It is often obferved of wits, that they will lofe their beft friend for the fake of a joke. Candour may difcover, that it is their greater degree of the love of fame, not the lefs degree of their benevolence, which is the caufe.

XX.

People in high or in diftinguifhed life ought to have a greater circumfpection in regard to their moft trivial actions. For inftance, I faw Mr Pope,—and what was he doing when you faw him? —why, to the beft of my memory, he was picking his nofe.

XXI.

Even Joe Miller in his jefts has an eye to poetical juftice; generally gives the victory or turns the laugh on the fide of merit: No fmall compliment to mankind.

XXII.

To fay a perfon writes a good ftyle, is originally as pedantic an expreffion, as to fay he plays a good fiddle.

XXIII.

The firft line of Virgil feems to patter like an hail-ftorm —*Tityre, tu patulae,* &c.

XXIV.

XXIV.

THE vanity and extreme felf-love of the French is no where more obfervable than in their authors; and among thefe, in none more than Boileau, who, befides his rhodomontades, preferves every the moft infipid reading in his notes, though he have removed it from the text for the fake of one ever fo much better.

XXV.

THE writer who gives us the beft idea of what may be called *the genteel in ftyle and manner of writing*, is, in my opinion, my Lord Shaftefbury; then Mr Addifon and Dr Swift.

A PLAIN narrative of any remarkable fact, emphatically related, has a more ftriking effect without the author's comment.

XXVI.

LONG periods and fhort feem analogous to Gothic and modern ftair-cafes. The former were of fuch a fize as our heads and legs could barely command; the latter fuch that they might command half a dozen.

I THINK nothing truly poetic, at leaft no poetry worth compofing, that does not ftrongly affect one's paffions: and this is but flenderly effected by fables, allegories, and lies.

Incredulus odi. Hor.

XXVII.

A PREFACE very frequently contains fuch a piece of criticifm, as tends to countenance and eftablifh the peculiarities of the piece.

XXVIII.

XXVIII.

I HATE a ftyle, as I do a garden, that is wholly flat and regular ; that flides along like an eel, and never rifes to what one can call an inequality.

XXIX.

It is obvious to difcover that imperfections of one kind have a vifible tendency to produce perfections of another. Mr Pope's bodily difadvantages muft incline him to a more laborious cultivation of his talent, without which he forefaw that he muft have languifhed in obfcurity. The advantages of perfon are a good deal eflential to popularity in the grave world as well as the gay. Mr Pope, by an unwearied application to poetry, became not only the favourite of the learned, but alfo of the ladies.

XXX.

Pope, I think, never once mentions Prior, though Prior fpeaks fo handfomely of Pope in his Alma. One might imagine, that the latter, indebted as he was to the former for fuch numberlefs beauties, fhould have readily repaid this poetical obligation. This can only be imputed to pride or party-cunning ; in other words, to fome modification of felfifhnefs.

XXXI.

Virgil never mentions Horace, though indebted to him for two very well-natured compliments.

XXXII.

XXXII.

Pope feems to me the moft correct writer fince Virgil, the greateft genius only fince Dryden.

XXXIII.

No one was ever more fortunate than Mr Pope in a judicious choice of his poetical fubjects.

XXXIV.

Pope's talent lay remarkably in what one may naturally enough term the condenfation of thoughts. I think no other Englifh poet ever brought fo much fenfe into the fame number of lines with equal fmoothnefs, eafe, and poetical beauty. Let him who doubts of this perufe his Effay on Man with attention. Perhaps this was a talent from which he could not eafily have fwerved: perhaps he could not have fufficiently rarefied his thoughts, to produce that flimzinefs which is required in a ballad or love-fong. His monfter of Ragufa and his tranflations from Chaucer have fome little tendency to invalidate this obfervation.

XXXV.

I durst not have cenfured Mr Pope's writings in his lifetime, you fay. True. A writer furrounded with all his fame, engaging with another that is hardly known, is a man in armour attacking another in his night-gown and flippers.

XXXVI.

Pope's religion is often found very advantageous to his defcriptive talents, as it is no doubt embellished with the moft pompous fcenes, and oftentatious imagery.. *Vid.*

When from the tenfer clouds of, &c.

XXXVII.

Pope has made the utmoft advantage of alliteration, regulating it by the paufe with the utmoft fuccefs :

Die, and endow a college or a cat, &c. &c.

It is an eafy kind of beauty. Dryden feems to have borrowed it from Spenfer.

XXXVIII.

Pope has publifhed fewer foibles than any other poet that is equally voluminous.

XXXIX.

It is no doubt extremely poffible to form an Englifh profody ; but to a good ear it were almoft fuperfluous, and to a bad one ufelefs ; this laft being, I believe, never joined with a poetic genius. It may be joined with wit; it may be connected with found judgment; but is furely never united with tafte, which is the life and foul of poetry.

XL.

Rhymes, in elegant poetry, fhould confift of fyllables that are long in pronunciation; fuch as *are, ear, ire, ore, your*; in which a nice ear will find more agreeablenefs than in thefe *gnat, net, knit, knot, nut.*

XLI.

XLI.

THERE is a vaſt beauty (to me) in uſing a word of a particular nature in the eighth and ninth ſyllables of an Engliſh verſe. I mean what is virtually a dactyl. For inſtance,

And pikes, the tyrants of the wat'ry plains.

Let any perſon of an ear ſubſtitute *liquid* inſtead of *wat'ry,* and he will find the diſadvantage. Mr Pope (who has improved our verſification through a judicious diſpoſition of the pauſe) ſeems not enough aware of this beauty.

XLII.

As to the frequent uſe of alliteration, it has probably had its day.

XLIII.

IT has ever a good effect when the ſtreſs of the thought is laid upon that word which the voice moſt naturally pronounces with an emphaſis.

I nunc, et verſus tecum meditare, &c. Hor.
Quam vellent aethere in alto.
Nunc et pauperiem, &c. Virg.
O fortunati, quorum jam mœnia, &c. Virg.
At regina gravi jamdudum, &c. Virg.

Virgil, whoſe very metre appears to affect one's paſſions, was a maſter of this ſecret.

XLIV.

THERE are numbers in the world who do not

M 2

want

want fenfe to make a figure, fo much as an opinion of their own abilities to put them upon recording their obfervations, and allowing them the fame importance which they do to thofe which others print.

XLV.

A good writer cannot with the utmoft ftudy produce fome thoughts which will flow from a bad one with eafe, and precipitation. The reverfe is alfo true. A bad writer, &c.

XLVI.

" Great wits have fhort memories," is a proverb, and as fuch has undoubtedly fome foundation in nature. The cafe feems to be, that men of genius forget things of common concern, unimportant facts and circumftances, which make no flight impreffion in every-day minds. But fure it will be found that all wit depends on memory; i. e. on the recollection of paffages either to illuftrate, or contraft with, any prefent occafion. It is probably the fate of a common underftanding, to forget the very things which the man of wit remembers. But an oblivion of thofe things which almoft every one remembers, renders his cafe the more remarkable, and thus explains the myftery.

XLVII.

Prudes allow no quarter to fuch ladies as have fallen a facrifice to the gentle paffions, either becaufe themfelves, being borne away by the malignant ones, perhaps never felt the other fo powerful as to occafion them any difficulty ; or
becaufe

becaufe no one has tempted them to tranfgrefs that way themfelves. It is the fame cafe with fome critics, with regard to the errours of ingenious writers.

XLVIII.

It feems with wit and good-nature, *Utrum horum mavis accipe.* Tafte and good-nature are univerfally connected.

XLIX.

Voiture's compliments to ladies are honeft on account of their excefs.

L.

Poetry and confumptions are the moft flattering of difeafes.

LI.

Every perfon infenfibly fixes upon fome degree of refinement in his difcourfe, fome meafure of thought which he thinks worth exhibiting. It is wife to fix this pretty high, although it occafions one to talk the lefs.

LII.

Some men ufe no other means to acquire refpect, than by infifting on it; and it fometimes anfwers their purpofe, as it does an highwayman's in regard to money.

LIII.

There is nothing exerts a genius fo much as writing plays: the reafon is, that the writer puts himfelf in the place of every perfon that fpeaks.

LIV.

Perfect characters in a poem make but lit-

M 3

tle

tle better figure than regular hills, perpendicu-
lar trees, uniform rocks, and level sheets of water, in the formation of a landscape. The reason is, they are not natural, and moreover want
variety.

LV.

TRIFLES discover a character more than actions of importance. In regard to the former,
a person is off his guard, and thinks it not material to use disguise. It is, to me, no imperfect
hint towards the discovery of a man's character,
to say he looks as though you might be certain
of finding a pin upon his sleeve.

LVI.

A GRAMMARIAN speaks of first and second
person; a poet of Celia and Corydon; a ma-
thematician of A. and B.; a lawyer of Nokes
and Styles: The very quintessence of pedantry!

LVII.

SHAKESPEAR makes his very bombast answer his purpose, by the persons he chuses to
utter it.

LVIII.

A POET, till he arrives at thirty, can see no
other good than a poetical reputation. About
that æra he begins to discover some other.

THE plan of Spenser's Fairy-queen appears
to me very imperfect; his imagination, though
very extensive, yet somewhat less so, perhaps,
than is generally allowed, if one considers the
facility of realising and equipping forth the vir-

tues and vices. His metre has fome advantages, though in many refpects exceptionable; his good-nature vifible through every part of his poem; his conjunction of the Pagan and Chriftian fcheme (as he introduces the deities of both acting fimultaneoufly) wholly inexcufable. Much art and judgment are difcovered in parts, and but little in the whole. One may entertain fome doubt whether the perufal of his monftrous defcriptions be not as prejudicial to true tafte, as it is advantageous to the extent of imagination. Spenfer, to be fure, expands the laft, but then he expands it beyond its due limits. After all, there are many favourite paffages in his Fairy-queen, which will be inftances of a great and cultivated genius mifapplied.

LIX.

A poet that fails in writing, becomes often a morofe critic. The weak and infipid white-wine makes at length a figure in vinegar.

LX.

People of fortune, perhaps, covet the acquaintance of eftablifhed writers, not fo much upon account of the focial pleafure, as the credit of it: the former would induce them to chufe perfons of lefs capacities, and tempers more conformable.

LXI.

Language is to the underftanding what a genteel motion is to the body, a very great advantage. But a perfon may be fuperiour to another in underftanding, that has not an equal dignity

nity

nity of expreſſion; and a man may boaſt an hand-
ſomer figure, that is inferiour to another in regard to motion.

LXII.

THE words *no more* have a ſingular pathos;
reminding us at once of paſt pleaſure, and
the future excluſion of it.

LXIII.

EVERY ſingle obſervation that is publiſhed by
a man of genius, be it ever ſo trivial, ſhould be
eſteemed of importance, becauſe he ſpeaks from
his own impreſſions; whereas common men pu-
bliſh common things, which they have, perhaps,
gleaned from frivolous writers.

LXIV.

IT is providential that our affection diminiſhes
in proportion as our friends power increaſes.
Affection is of leſs importance whenever a perſon can ſupport himſelf. It is on this account
that younger brothers are often beloved more
than their elders, and that Benjamin is the favourite. We may trace the ſame law throughout the animal creation.

LXV.

THE time of life when fancy predominates, is
youth; the ſeaſon when judgment decides beſt,
is age. Poets, therefore, are always, in reſpect
of their diſpoſition, younger than other perſons:
A circumſtance that gives the latter part of their
lives ſome inconſiſtency. The cool phlegmatic
tribe diſcover it in the former.

LXVI.

LXVI.

ONE fometimes meets with inftances of genteel abruption in writers; but I wonder it is not ufed more frequently, as it has a prodigious effect upon the reader. For inftance (after Falftaff's difappointment in ferving Shallow at court)

> *Mafter Shallow, I owe you a thoufand pounds.——*
>
> Shakefpear.

WHEN Pandulph commanded Philip of France to proceed no farther againft England, but to fheath the fword he had drawn at the Pope's own inftigation:

> *Now it had already coft Philip eighty thoufand pound in preparations——*

AFTER the detail of King John's abject fubmiffion to the Pope's legate,

> *Now John was hated and defpifed before.*

BUT, perhaps, the ftrongeft of all may be taken from the Scripture. (Conclufion of a chapter in St John)

> *Now Barabbas was a robber.——*

LXVII.

A POET hurts himfelf by writing profe, as a race-horfe hurts his motions by condefcending to draw in a team.

LXVIII.

LXVIII.

THE fuperiour politenefs of the French is in nothing more difcernible than in the phrafes ufed by them and us to exprefs an affair being in agitation. The former fays, *fur la tapis;* the latter, *upon the anvil.* Does it not fhew alfo the fincerity and ferious face with which we enter upon bufinefs, and the negligent and jaunty air with which they perform even the moft important ?

LXIX.

THERE are two qualities adherent to the moft ingenious authors; I do not mean without exception; a decent pride that will admit of no fervility, and a fheepifh bafhfulnefs that keeps their worth concealed; the *fuperbia quaefita meritis,* and the *malus pudor* of Horace. The one will not fuffer them to make advances to the great; the other difguifes that merit for which the great would feek out them. Add to thefe the frequent indolence of fpeculative tempers.

LXX.

A POETICAL genius feems the moft elegant of youthful accomplifhments; but it is entirely a youthful one. Flights of fancy, gaiety of behaviour, fprightlinefs of drefs, and a blooming afpect, confpire very amicably to their mutual embellifhment : but the poetic talent has no more to do with age, than it would avail his Grace of Canterbury to have a knack at country-dances, or a genius for a catch.

LXXI.

LXXI.

THE moſt obſequious muſes, like the fondeſt and moſt willing courtezans, ſeldom leave us any reaſon to boaſt much of their favours.

LXXII.

IF you write an original piece, you wonder no one ever thought of the beſt of ſubjects before you ; if a tranſlation, of the beſt authors.

LXXIII.

THE ancient poets ſeem to value themſelves greatly upon their power of perpetuating the fame of their contemporaries. Indeed the circum-ſtance that has fixed their language, has been the only means of verifying ſome of their vain-glorious prophecies. Otherwiſe the hiſtorians appear more equal to the taſk of conferring im-mortality. An hiſtory will live, though writ-ten ever ſo indifferently ; and is generally leſs ſuſpected than the rhetoric of the muſes.

LXXIV.

I WONDER authors do not diſcover how much more elegant it is to fix their name to the end of their preface, or any introductory addreſs, than to the title-page. It is, perhaps, for the ſake of an F. R. S. or an LL. D. at the end of it.

LXXV.

IT ſhould ſeem, the many lies diſcernible in books of travels, may be owing to accounts col-lected from improper people. Were one to give a character of the Engliſh from what the vulgar

act

act and believe, it would convey * a strange idea of the Englifh underftanding.

LXXVI.

Might not the poem on the Seafons have been rendered more *uni*, by giving out the defign of nature in the beginning of winter, and afterwards confidering all the varieties of feafon as means aiming at one end?

LXXVII.

Critics muft excufe me, if I compare them to certain animals called affes, who by gnawing vines originally taught the great advantage of pruning them.

LXXVIII.

Every good poet includes a critic; the reverfe will not hold.

LXXIX.

We want a word to exprefs the *hofpes* or *hofpita* of the ancients; among them, perhaps, the moft refpectable of all characters, yet with us tranflated *hoft*, which we apply alfo to an inn-keeper. Neither have we any word to exprefs *amica*, as if we thought a woman always was fomewhat more or lefs than a friend.

LXXX.

I know not where any Latin author ufes *ignotos* otherwife than as obfcure: " Perfons," as the modern phrafe implies, " whom nobody

---

* Miffionaries clap a tail to every Indian nation that diflikes them.

" knows."

" knows." Yet it is uſed differently on Mrs
L———'s monument.

LXXXI.

THE philoſopher who conſidered the world as
one vaſt animal, could eſteem himſelf no other
than a louſe upon the back of it.

LXXXII.

ORATORS and ſtage-coachmen, when the one
wants arguments, and the other a coat of arms,
adorn their cauſe and their coaches with rhetoric
and flower-pots.

LXXXIII.

IT is idle to be much aſſiduous in the peruſal
of inferiour poetry. Homer, Virgil, and Horace,
give the true taſte in compoſition ; and a perſon's own imagination ſhould be able to ſupply
the reſt.

IN the ſame manner it is ſuperfluous to purſue
inferiour degrees of fame. One truly ſplendid
action, or one well-finiſhed compoſition, includes
more than all the reſults from more trivial performances. I mean this for perſons who make
fame their only motive.

VERY few ſentiments are proper to be put in
a perſon's mouth, during the firſt attack of
grief.

EVERY thing diſguſts but mere ſimplicity ;
the ſcriptural writers deſcribe their heroes uſing
only ſome ſuch phraſe as this : " Alas my bro-
" ther ; O Abſalom my ſon ! my ſon !" &c.
The lamentation of Saul over Jonathan is more
diffuſe, but at the ſame time entirely ſimple.

ANGLING is literally defcribed by Martial :

—tremula pifcem deducere feta.

FROM *ictum foedus* feems to come the Englifh phrafe and cuftom of *ftriking a bargain.*

I LIKE Ovid's Amours better than his Epi-ftles. There feems a greater variety of natural thoughts : whereas when one has read the fub-ject of one of his epiftles, one forefees what it will produce in a writer of his imagination.

THE plan of his Elegies for the moft part is well defigned—the anfwers of Sabinus, nothing.

NECESSITY may be the mother of lucrative invention, but is the death of poetical.

IF a perfon fufpects his phrafe to be fomewhat too familiar and abject, it were proper he fhould accuftom himfelf to compofe in blank verfe : but let him be much upon his guard againft Ancient Piftol's phrafeology.

PROVIDENCE feems altogether impartial in the difpenfation which beftows riches upon one, and a contempt of riches upon another.

RESPECT is the general end for which riches, power, place, title, and fame, are implicitly de-fired. When one is poffeffed of the end through any one of thefe means, is it not wholly unphi-lofophical to covet the remainder ?

LORD Shaftefbury, in the genteel management of fome familiar ideas, feems to have no equal. He difcovers an eloignment from vulgar phrafes much becoming a perfon of quality. His fketches fhould be ftudied like thofe of Raphael. His

Inquiry

Inquiry is one of the shortest and clearest sy-
stems of morality.

The question is, Whether you distinguish
me, because you have better sense than other
people; or whether you seem to have better sense
than other people, because you distinguish me?

One feels the same kind of disgust in reading the Roman history, which one does in no-
vels, or even epic poetry. We too easily foresee
to whom the victory will fall. The hero, the
knight-errant, and the Roman are too seldom
overcome.

The elegance and dignity of the Romans is in
nothing more conspicuous than in their answers
to ambassadors.

There is an important omission in most of
our grammar-schools, through which what we
read either of fabulous or real history, leaves either faint or confused impressions. I mean the
neglect of old geographic maps. Were maps of
ancient Greece, Sicily, Italy, &c. in use there,
the knowledge we there acquire would not want
to be renewed afterwards, as is now generally
the case.

A person of a pedantic turn will spend five
years in translating, and contending for the beauties of a worse poem than he might write in five
weeks himself. There seem to be authors who
wish to sacrifice their whole character of genius
to that of learning.

Boileau has endeavoured to prove in one of
his admirable satires, that man has no manner of
pretence to prefer his faculties before those of

the

the brute creation. Oldham has tranflated him ;
my Lord Rochefter has imitated him ; and even
Mr Pope declares,

That reafon raife o'er inftinĉt how you can,
In this 'tis God directs ; in that 'tis man.

INDEED the Effay on Man abounds with illu-
ftrations of this maxim; and it is amazing to find
how many plaufible reafons may be urged to
fupport it. It feems evident, that our itch of
reafoning, and fpirit of curiofity precludes more
happinefs than it can poffibly advance. What
numbers of difeafes are entirely artificial things ?
far from the ability of a brute to contrive. We
difrelifh and deny ourfelves cheap and natural
gratifications, through fpeculative prefciences and
doubts about the future. We cannot difcover
the defigns of our Creator. We fhould learn
then of brutes to be eafy under our ignorance,
and happy in thofe objeĉts that feem intended
obvioufly for our happinefs ; not overlook the
flowers of the garden, and foolifhly perplex ourfelves with the intricacies of the labyrinth.

I WISH but two editions of all books whatfoever. One of the fimple text, publifhed by a
fociety of able hands ; another with the various readings and remarks of the ableft commentators.

To endeavour, all one's days, to fortify our
minds with learning and philofophy, is to fpend
fo much in armour that one has nothing left to
defend.

IF one would think with philofophers, one
must

muſt converſe but little with the vulgar. Theſe by their very number will force a perſon into a fondneſs for appearance, a love of money, a deſire of power, and other plebeian paſſions ; objects which they admire, becauſe they have no ſhare in ; and have not learning to ſupply the place of experience.

Livy, the moſt elegant and principal of the Roman hiſtorians, was, perhaps, as ſuperſtitious as the moſt unlearned plebeian.. We ſee he never is deſtitute of appearances, accurately deſcribed, and ſolemnly aſſerted, to ſupport particular events by the interpoſition of exploded deities. The puerile attention to chickens feeding in a morning—and then a· piece of gravity : *Parva ſunt haec, ſed parva iſta non contemnenda ; majores noſtri maximam hanc rem fecerunt..*

· It appears from the Roman hiſtorians, that the Romans had a peculiar veneration for the fortunate. Their epithet *Felix* ſeems ever to imply a favourite of the gods. I am miſtaken, or modern Rome has generally acted in an oppoſite manner. Numbers amongſt them have been canonized upon the ſingle merit of misfortunes.

How different appears ancient and modern dialogue, on account of the ſuperficial ſubjects . upon which we now generally converſe ! Add to this the ceremonial of modern times,. and the number of titles with which ſome kings clog and encumber converſation.

The celebrated boldneſs of an eaſtern metaphor is, I believe, ſometimes allowed it, for the inconſiderable ſimilitude it bears to its ſubject.

The

THE ftyle of letters, perhaps, fhould not rife higher than the ftyle of refined converfation.

LOVE-VERSES, written without real paffion, are often the moft naufeous of all conceits. Thofe written from the heart will ever bring to mind that delightful feafon of youth, and poetry, and love.

VIRGIL gives one fuch exceffive pleafure in his writings, beyond any other writer, by uniting the moft perfect harmony of metre, with the moft pleafing ideas, or images.

Qualem virgineo demeffum pollice florem.

And

Argentum Pariufve lapis ——

With a thoufand better inftances.

NOTHING tends fo much to produce drunkennefs, or even madnefs, as the frequent ufe of parenthefes in converfation.

FEW greater images of impatience, than a general feeing his brave army over-matched and cut to pieces, and looking out continually to fee his ally approach with forces to his affiftance. See Shakefpear.

When my dear Percy, when my heart's dear Harry
Caft many a northward look to fee his father
Bring up his pow'rs — but he did look in vain.

BOOKS,

B O O K S, &c.

SIMILES drawn from odd circumftances and effects ftrangely accidental, bear a near relation to falfe wit. The beft inftance of the kind is that celebrated line of Waller :

He grafp'd at love, and fill'd his hand with bays.

VIRGIL difcovers lefs wit, and more tafte than any writer in the world. — Some inftances,

—— *longumque bibebat amorem.*

WHAT Lucretius fays of the *edita doctrinae fapientum templa,* —— " the temples of philofo- " phers," —— appears in no fenfe more applicable than to a fnug and eafy chariot :

Difpicere unde queas alios, paffimque videre
Errare, atque viam palantes quaerere vitae.

i. e. From whence you may look down upon foot-paffengers, fee them wandering on each fide you, and pick their way through the dirt.

———————————————*ferioufly*
From learning's tow'ring height to gaze around,
And fee plebeian fpirits range below.

THERE is a fort of mafonry in poetry, wherein the paufe reprefents the joints of building ;
which.

which ought in every line and courfe to have their difpofition varied.

The difference betwixt a witty writer and a writer of tafte is chiefly this. The former is negligent what ideas he introduces, fo he joins them furprifingly.——The latter is principally careful what images he introduces, and ftudies fimplicity rather than furprife in his manner of introduction.

It may in fome meafure account for the dif-ference of tafte in the reading of books, to con-fider the difference of our ears for mufic. One is not pleafed without a perfect melody of ftyle, be the fenfe what it will : another, of no ear for mufic, gives to fenfe its full weight without any deduction on account of harfhnefs.

Harmony of period, and melody of ftyle have greater weight than is generally imagined in the judgment we pafs upon writing and writers. As a proof of this, let us reflect, what texts of fcrip-ture, what lines in poetry, or what periods we muft remember and quote, either in verfe or profe, and we fhall find them to be only mufical ones.

I wonder the ancient mythology never fhews Apollo enamoured of Venus, confidering the remarkable deference that wit has paid to beauty in all ages. The Orientals act more confonantly, when they fuppofe the nightingale enamoured of the rofe, the moft harmonious bird of the faireft and moft delightful flower.

Hope is a flatterer ; but the moft upright of
all

all parafites, for fhe frequents the poor man's hut, as well as the palace of his fuperiour.

What is termed humour in profe, I conceive, would be confidered as burlefque in poetry : of which inftances may be given.

Perhaps, burlefque may be divided into fuch as turns chiefly upon the thought, and fuch as depends more upon the expreffion : or we may add a third kind, confifting in thoughts ridiculoufly dreffed in language much above or below their dignity.

The Splendid Shilling of Mr Philips, and the Hudibras of Butler, are the moft obvious inftances.   Butler, however, depended much upon the ludicrous effect of his double rhymes.   In other refpects, to declare my own fentiments, he is rather a witty writer than an humorous one.

Scenes below verfe, merely verfified, lay claim to a degree of humour.

Swift in poetry deferves a place fomewhere betwixt Butler and Horace.   He has the wit of the former, and the graceful negligence which we find in the latter's epiftles and fatires.   I believe few people difcover lefs humour in Don Quixote than myfelf.   For befide the general famenefs of adventure, whereby it is eafy to forefee what he will do on moft occafions, it is not fo eafy to raife a laugh from the wild achievements of a madman.   The natural paffion in that cafe is pity, with fome fmall portion of mirth at moft.   Sancho's character is indeed comic, and, were it removed from the romance, would dif-

cover-

cover how little there was of humour in the character of Don Quixote.

IT is a fine ftroke of Cervantes, when Sancho, fick of his government, makes no anfwer to his comforters, but aims directly at his fhoes and ftockings.

O R

Of MEN and MANNERS.

I.

THE arguments againſt pride drawn ſo frequently by our clergy from the general
infirmity, circumſtances, and cataſtrophe of our
nature, are extremely trifling and inſignificant.
Man is not proud as a ſpecies, but as an individual ; not as comparing himſelf with other beings, but with his fellow-creatures.

II.

I HAVE often thought that people draw many
of their ideas of agreeableneſs in regard to proportion, colour, &c. from their own perſons.

III.

IT is happy enough that the ſame vices which
impair one's fortune, frequently ruin our con-
ſtitution, that the one may not ſurvive the
other.

IV.

DEFERENCE often ſhrinks and withers as
much upon the approach of intimacy, as the
ſenſitive plant does upon the touch of one's
finger.

V.

THE word *folly* is, perhaps, the prettieſt word
in the language. *Amuſement* and *diverſion* are
good well-meaning words : but *paſtime* is what
never ſhould be uſed but in a bad ſenſe. It is vile
to ſay ſuch a thing is agreeable, becauſe it helps
to paſs the time away.

VI.

VI.

DANCING in the rough is one of the moſt natural expreſſions of joy, and coincides with jump-
ing.   When it is regulated, it is merely *cum ra-
tione inſanire.*

VII.

A PLAIN, downright, open-hearted fellow's
converſation is as inſipid, ſays Sir Plume, as a
play without a plot ; it does not afford one the
amuſement of thinking.

VIII.

THE fortunate have many paraſites. Hope is
the only one that vouchſafes attendance upon
the wretched and the beggar.

IX.

A MAN of genius miſtaking his talent loſes the
advantage of being diſtinguiſhed; a fool of being
undiſtinguiſhed.

X.

JEALOUSY is the fear or apprehenſion of ſuperiority; envy our uneaſineſs under it.

XI.

WHAT ſome people term *freedom* is nothing
elſe than a liberty of ſaying and doing diſagree-
able things.   It is but carrying the notion a little
higher, and it would require us to break and
have a head broken reciprocally without offence.

XII.

I CANNOT ſee why people are aſhamed to acknowledge their paſſion for popularity. The love
of popularity is the love of being beloved.

XIII.

XIII.

THE ridicule with which fome people affect to triumph over their fuperiours, is as though the moon under an eclipfe fhould pretend to laugh at the fun.

XIV.

ZEALOUS men are ever difplaying to you the ftrength of their belief, while judicious men are fhewing you the grounds of it.

XV.

I CONSIDER your very tefty and quarrelfome people in the fame light as I do a loaded gun, which may by accident go off and kill one.

XVI.

I AM afraid humility to genius is as an extin-guifher to a candle.

XVII.

MANY perfons, when exalted, affume an info-lent humility, who behaved before with an info-lent haughtinefs.

XVIII.

MEN are fometimes accufed of pride, merely becaufe their accufers would be proud themfelves, if they were in their places.

XIX.

MEN of fine parts, they fay, are often proud ; I anfwer, dull people are feldom fo, and both act upon an appearance of reafon.

XX.

IT was obferved of a moft accomplifhed lady, that fhe was withal fo very modeft, that one fome-

times thought fhe neglected the praifes of her
wit, becaufe fhe could depend on thofe of her
beauty ; at other times that fhe flighted thofe of
her beauty, knowing fhe might rely on thofe of
her wit.

XXI.

THE only difference betwixt wine and ale,
feems to be that of chemic and galenic medicines.

XXII.

IT is the reduplication or accumulation of
compliments that gives them their agreeablenefs :
I mean, when feeming to wander from the fubject, you return to it again with greater force.
As a common inftance : " I wifh it was capable
" of a precife demonftration how much I efteem,
" love, and honour you, beyond all the rich, the
" gay, the great of this fublunary fphere : but
" I believe that both divines and laymen will
" agree, that the fublimeft and moft valuable
" truths are oftentimes leaft capable of demon-
" ftration."

XXIII.

IT is a noble piece of policy that is ufed in
fome arbitrary governments, (but fuitable to none
other), to inftill it into the minds of the people,
that their Great Duke knoweth all things.

XXIV.

IN an heavy oppreffive atmofphere, when the
fpirits fink too low, the beft cordial is to read
over all the letters of one's friends.

XXV.

XXV.

PRIDE and modefty are fometimes found to unite together in the fame character; and the mixture is as falutary as that of wine and water. The worft combination I know is that of avarice and pride, as the former naturally obftructs the good that pride eventually produces. What I mean is, expenfe.

XXVI.

A GREAT many tunes, by a variety of circum-rotatory flourifhes, put one in mind of a lark's defcent to the ground.

XXVII.

PEOPLE frequently ufe this expreffion, " I am " inclined to think fo and fo ;" not confidering that they are then fpeaking the moft literal of all truths.

XXVIII.

THE firft part of a news-paper which an ill-natured man examines, is, the lift of bankrupts, and the bills of mortality.

XXIX.

THE chief thing which induces men of fenfe to ufe airs of fuperiority, is the contemplation of coxcombs ; that is, conceited fools, who would otherwife run away with the men of fenfe's privileges.

XXX.

To be entirely ingroffed by antiquity, and as it were eaten up with ruft, is a bad compliment to the prefent age.

XXXI.

XXXI.

Ask to borrow fix-pence of the Mufes, and they tell you at prefent they are out of cafh, but hereafter they will furnifh you with five thoufand pounds.

XXXII.

The argument againft reftraining our paffions, becaufe we fhall not have it always in our power to gratify them, is much ftronger for their reftraint, than it is for their indulgence.

XXXIII.

Few men that would caufe refpect and diftance merely, can fay any thing by which their end will be fo effectually anfwered as by filence.

XXXIV.

There is nothing more univerfally commended than a fine day; the reafon is, that people can commend it without envy.

XXXV.

One may, modeftly enough, calculate one's appearance for refpect upon the road, where refpect and convenience fo remarkably coincide.

XXXVI.

Although a man cannot procure himfelf a title at pleafure, he may vary the appellation he goes by confiderably; as, from Tom, to Mr Thomas, to Mr Mufgrove, to Thomas Mufgrove, Efquire; and this by a behaviour of referve, or familiarity.

XXXVII.

For a man of genius to condefcend in conver-

fation

fation with vulgar people, gives the fenfation that a tall man feels on being forced to ftoop in a low room.

XXXVIII.

There is nothing more univerfally prevalent than flattery. Perfons who difcover the flatter-er, do not always difapprove him, becaufe he imagines them confiderable enough to deferve his applications. It is a tacit fort of compliment, that he efteems them to be fuch as it is worth his while to flatter.

And when I tell him he hates flattery,
He fays he does, being then moft flattered.
Shakespear.

XXXIX.

A person has fometimes more public than private merit. Honorio and his family wore mourning for their anceftor ; but that of all the world was internal and fincere.

Your plain domeftic people, who talk of their humility and home-felt fatisfactions, will in the fame breath difcover how much they envy a fhining character. How is this con-fiftent ?

You are prejudiced, fays Pedanticus ; I will not take your word or your character of that man.—But the grounds of my prejudice are the fource of my accufation.

A proud man's intimates are generally more attached to him, than the man of merit and hu-

O 3

mility

mility can pretend his to be. The reafon is, the former pays a greater compliment· in his conde-fcenfion.

THE fituation of a king is fo far from being miferable, as pedants term it, that, if a perfon have magnanimity, it is the happieft I know; as he has affuredly the moft opportunities of diftinguifhing merit, and conferring obligations.

XL.

Contemptae dominus fplendidior rei.

A MAN, a gentleman, evidently appears more confiderable by feeming to defpife his fortune, than a citizen and mechanic by his endeavours to magnify it.

XLI.

WHAT man of fenfe, for the benefit of coal-mines, would be plagued with colliers converfa-tion ?

XLII.

MODESTY makes large amends for the pain it gives the perfons who labour under it, by the prejudice it affords every worthy perfon in their favour.

XLIII.

THIRD thoughts often coincide with the firft, and are generally the beft grounded. We firft relifh nature and the country, then artificial amufements and the city; then become impatient to retire to the country again.

XLIV.

WHILE we labour to fubdue our paffions, we fhould take care not to extinguifh them. Sub-

duing

duing our paffions is difengaging ourfelves from the world ; to which, however, whilft we refide in it, we muft always bear relation ; and we may detach ourfelves to fuch a degree as to pafs an ufelefs and infipid life, which we were not meant to do. Our exiftence here is at leaft one part of a fyftem.

A man has generally the good or ill qualities which he attributes to mankind.

XLV.

Anger and the thirft of revenge are a kind of fever ; fighting and law-fuits, bleeding, at leaft an evacuation. The latter occafions a diffi- pation of money ; the former, of thofe fiery fpirits which caufe a preternatural fermenta- tion.

XLVI.

Were a man of pleafure to arrive at the full extent of his feveral wifhes, he muft immediately feel himfelf miferable. It is one fpecies of de- fpair to have no room to hope for any addition to one's happinefs.

His following wifh muft then be to wifh he had fome frefh object for his wifhes : A ftrong argument that our minds and bodies were both meant to be for ever active.

XLVII.

I have feen one evil underneath the fun which gives me particular mortification.

The referve or fhinefs of men of fenfe gene- rally confines them to a fmall acquaintance ; and they find numbers their avowed enemies, the

fimilarity

fimilarity of whofe taftes, had fortune brought them once acquainted, would have rendered them their fondeft friends.

XLVIII.

A MERE relator of matters of fact, is fit only for an evidence in a court of juftice.

XLIX.

IF a man be of fuperiour dignity to a woman, a woman is furely as much fuperiour to a man that is effeminated. Lily's rule in the grammar has well enough adjufted this fubordination: " The mafculine is more worthy than the femi- " nine, and the feminine more worthy than the " neuter."

L.

A GENTLEMAN of fortune will be often com- plaining of taxes, that his eftate is inconfider- able, that he can never make fo much of it as the world is ready to imagine. A mere citizen, on the other hand, is always aiming to fhew his riches ; fays, that he employs fo many hands, he keeps his wife a chaife and one, and talks much of his Chinefe ornaments at his paltry cake-houfe in the country. They both aim at praife, but of a very diftinct kind. Now, fup- pofing the cit worth as much in money as the other is in land, the gentleman furely chufes the better method of oftentation, who confiders him- felf as fomewhat fuperiour to his fortune, than he who feems to look up at his fortune, and con- fequently fets himfelf beneath it.

LI.

LI.

THE only kind of revenge which a man of fenfe need take upon a fcoundrel, is, by a feries of worthy behaviour, to force him to admire and efteem his enemy, and yet irritate his animofity, by declining a reconciliation ; as Sir John Fal-ftaff might fay, turning even quarrels to commodity.

LII.

IT is poffible, by means of glue, to connect two pieces of wood together ; by a powerful cement, to join marble ; by the mediation of a prieft, to unite a man and woman ; but of all affociations the moft effectual is betwixt an idiot and a knave. They become in a manner incorporate. The former feems fo framed to admire and idolize the latter, that the latter may feize and devour him as his proper prey.

LIII.

THE fame degree of penetration that fhews you another in the wrong, fhews him alfo, in refpect to that inftance, your inferiour. Hence the ob-fervation and the real fact, that people of clear heads are what the world calls opinionated.

LIV.

THERE is none can baffle men of fenfe, but fools, on whom they can make no impreffion.

LV.

THE regard one fhews œconomy, is like that we fhew an old aunt who is to leave us fomething at laft ; our behaviour on this account as much conftrained as that

Of

Of one well-studied in a sad ostent
To please his granam.

SHAKESPEAR.

LVI.

FASHION is a great restraint upon your perfons of taste and fancy; who would otherwife,
in the moft trifling inftances, be able to diftinguifh themfelves from the vulgar.

LVII.

A WRITER who pretends to polifh the human
underftanding, may beg by the fide of Rutter's
chariot, who fells a powder for the teeth.

LVIII.

THE difference there is betwixt honour and
honefty, feems to be chiefly in the motive. The
mere honeft man does that from duty, which the
man of honour does for the fake of character.

LIX.

THE proverb ought to run, " A fool and his
" words are foon parted ; a man of genius and
" his money."

LX.

A MAN of wit, genius, learning, is apt to
think it fomething hard, that men of no wit, no
genius, no learning, fhould have a greater fhare
of wealth and honours ; not confidering that
their own accomplifhment ought to be reckoned
to them as their equivalent. It is no reafon that
a perfon worth five thoufand pounds, fhould on
that account have a claim to twenty.

LXI.

LXI.

A wife ought in reality to love her hufband above all the world; but this preference I think fhould, in point of politenefs, be concealed. The reafon is, that it is difgufting to fee an amiable woman monopolized; and it is eafy by proper management to wave (all I contend for) the appearance.

LXII.

There are fome wounds given to reputation that are like the wounds of an envenomed arrow; where we irritate and enlarge the orifice, while we extract the bearded weapon; yet cannot the cure be completed otherwife.

LXIII.

Amongst all the vain-glorious profeffors of humility, you find none that will not difcover how much they envy a fhining character; and this either by cenfuring it themfelves, or fhewing a fatisfaction in fuch as do. Now, there is this advantage at leaft arifing from ambition, that it difpofes one to difregard a thoufand inftances of middling grandeur, and reduces one's emulation to the narrow circle of a few that blaze. It is hence a convenient difpofition in a country-place, where one is encompaffed with fuch as are merely richer, keep fine horfes, a table, footmen; make a decent figure as rural efquires; yet after all difcover no more than an every-day plebeian character. Thefe a perfon of little ambition might envy, but another of a more extenfive one may, in any kind of circumftances, difregard.

LXIV.

LXIV.

IT is with fome men as with fome horfes; what is efteemed fpirit in them proceeds from fear. This was undoubtedly the fource of that feeming fpirit difcovered by Tully in regard to his antagonift M. Anthony. He knew he muft deftroy him, or be deftroyed himfelf.

LXV.

THE fame qualities joined with virtue, often furnifh out a great man, which united with a different principle furnifh out an highwayman; I mean courage and ftrong paffions. And they may both join in the fame expreffion, though with a meaning fomething varied.———

Tentanda via eft qua me quoque poffum
Tollere humo.

i. e. " Be promoted or be hanged."

LXVI.

TRUE honour is to honefty, what the court of chancery is to common law.

LXVII.

MISERS, as death approaches, are heaping up a cheft of reafons to ftand more in awe of him.

LXVIII.

A MAN fooner finds out his own foibles in a ftranger, than any other foibles.

LXIX.

IT is favourable enough on the fide of learning, that if an hiftorian mentions a good author,

thor, it does not feem abfurd to ftyle him a great
man : whereas the fame phrafe would not be
allowed to a mere illiterate nobleman.

LXX.

IT is lefs wonderful to fee a wretched man
commence an hero, than an happy one.

LXXI.

AN high fpirit has often very different and
even contrary effects. It fometimes operates no
otherwife than like the *vis inertiae*; at others it
induces men to buftle and make their part good
among their fuperiours. As Mr Pope fays,

> *Some plunge in bufinefs, others fhave their
> crowns.*

IT is by no means lefs forcible, when it with-
draws a man from the company of thofe with
whom he cannot converfe on equal terms; it
leads him into folitude, that if he cannot appear
their equal, he may at leaft conceal his inferiority. It is fullen, obftinate, difdainful, haughty,
in no lefs a degree than the other; but is, perhaps, more genteel, and lefs citizen-like. Sometimes the other fucceeds, and then it is efteemed
preferable; but in cafe it fail, it not only expofes a perfon's meannefs, but his impatience under it; both of which the referved fpirit is able
to difguife—but then it ftands no chance of removing.

Pudor malus ulcera celat.

LXXII.

EVERY single instance of a friend's insincerity increases our dependence on the efficacy of money. It makes one covet what produces an external respect, when one is disappointed of that which is internal and sincere. This, perhaps, with decaying passions, contributes to render age covetous.

LXXIII.

WHEN physicians write of diseases, the prognostics and the diagnostics, the symptoms and the paroxysms, they give one fatal apprehensions for every ache about us. When they come to treat of medicines and applications, you seem to have no other difficulty but to decide by which means you would recover ; in short, to give the preference between a linctus and an apozem.

LXXIV.

ONE should no more trust to the skill of most apothecaries, than one would ask the opinion of their pestle and mortar ; yet both are useful in their way.

LXXV.

I BELIEVE there was never so reserved a solitary, but felt some degree of pleasure at the first glimpse of an human figure. The soul, however unconscious of its social bias in a croud, will in solitude feel some attraction towards the first person that we meet.

LXXVI.

IN courts, the motion of the body is easy, and
those

those of the soul constrained: in the country, the gestures of the body are constrained, and those of the soul supine and careless.

LXXVII.

ONE may easily enough guard against ambition till five and twenty.—It is not ambition's day.

LXXVIII.

IT should seem that indolence itself would incline a person to be honest; as it requires infinitely greater pains and contrivance to be a knave.

LXXIX.

PERHAPS rustics, boors, and esquires make a principal figure in the country, as inanimates are always allowed to be the chief figures in a landscape.

LXXX.

TITLES make a greater distinction than is almost tolerable to a British spirit. They almost vary the species; yet, as they are oftentimes conferred, seem not so much the reward, as the substitutes of merit.

LXXXI.

WHAT numbers live to the age of fifty or sixty years, yet if estimated by their merit, are not worth the price of a chicken the moment it is hatched!

LXXXII.

A LIAR begins with making falsehood appear

like

like truth, and ends with making truth itfelf appear like falfehood.

LXXXIII.

FOOLS are very often found united in the ftricteft intimacies, as the lighter kind of woods are the moft clofely glewed together.

LXXXIV.

PERSONS of great delicacy fhould know the certainty of the following truth. There are a-bundance of cafes which occafion fufpenfe, in which whatever they determine, they will repent of their determination; and this through a pro-penfity of human nature to fancy happinefs in thofe fchemes which it does not purfue.

LXXXV.

HIGH SPIRIT in a man is like a fword, which though worn to annoy his enemies, yet is often troublefome in a lefs degree to his friends. He can hardly wear it fo inoffenfively, but it is apt to incommode one or other of the company. It is more properly a loaded piftol, which acci-dent alone may fire, and kill one.

LXXXVI.

A MISER, if honeft, can be only honeft bare-weight.

AVARICE is the moft oppofite of all characters to that of God Almighty, whofe alone it is to give and not receive.

A MISER grows rich by feeming poor; an extravagant man grows poor by feeming rich.

A GRASHOPPER is, perhaps, the beft figure

for

for coat-armour of thofe who would be thought aborigines, agreeable to the Athenian ufe of them.

IMMODERATE affurance is perfect licen-tioufnefs.

WHEN a perfon is fo far engaged in a difpute as to wifh to get the victory, he ought ever to defift. The idea of conqueft will fo dazzle him, that it is hardly poffible he fhould difcern the truth.

I HAVE fometimes thought the mind fo cal-culated, that a fmall degree of force may impel it to a certain pitch of pleafure or of pain; be-yond which it will not pafs, by any impetus whatfoever.

I DOUBT whether it be not true, that we hate thofe faults moft in others which we are guilty of ourfelves.

A MAN of thorough fenfe fcarce admires even any one; but he muft be an idiot, that is the ad-mirer of a fool.

IT may be prudent to give up the more trivial parts of character for the amufement of the in-vidious; as a man willingly relinquifhes his filver to fave his gold from an highwayman. Better be ridiculed for an untoward peruke, than be attacked on the fcore of morals, as one would be rather pulled by the hair, than ftabbed to the heart.

VIRTUE feems to be nothing more than a no-tion confonant to the fyftem of things. Were a planet to fly from its orbit, it would reprefent a vitious man.

P 3

IT

IT is difficult not to be angry at beings we know incapable of acting otherwife than they do. One ought no more, if one reflects, to be angry at the ftupidity of a man than of a horfe, except it be vincible and voluntary, and yet the practice is otherwife.

PEOPLE fay, Do not regard what he fays, now he is in liquor. Perhaps it is the only time he ought to be regarded.

Aperit praecordia Liber.

PATIENCE is the panacea; but where does it grow, or who can fwallow it?

WITS uniformly exclaim againft fools, yet fools are their proper foil; and it is from them alone they can learn what figure themfelves make. Their behaviour naturally falls in with the generality, and furnifhes a better mirrour than that of artful people, who are fure enough to deceive you either on the favourable or. ill-natured fide.

WE fay he is a man of fenfe who acknowledges the fame truths that we do; that he is a man of tafte who allows the fame beauties. We confider him as a perfon of better fenfe and finer tafte, who difcerns more truths and more beauties in conjunction with ourfelves; but we allow neither appellation to the man who differs from us.

WE deal out our genuine efteem to our equals; our affection for thofe beneath us; and a reluctant fort of refpect to thofe that are above us,

GLORY

GLORY relaxes often, and debilitates the mind; cenfure ftimulates and contracts——both to an extreme. Simple fame is, perhaps, the proper medium.

PERSONS of new families do well to make magnificent funerals, fumptuous weddings, remarkable entertainments; to exhibit a number of fervants in rich and oftentatious liveries; and to take every public occafion of imprinting on the mob an habitual notion of their fuperiority. For fo is deference obtained from that quarter.

Stupet in titulis et imaginibus.

ONE fcarce fees how it is poffible for a country-girl or a country-fellow to preferve their chaftity. They have neither the philofophical pleafure of books, nor the luxurious pleafure of a table, nor the refined amufement of building, planting, drawing, or defigning, to divert their imagination from an object to which they feem continually to ftimulate it by provocative allufions. Add to this the health and vigour that are almoft peculiar to them.

I AM afraid there are many ladies who only exchange the pleafures of incontinence for the pleafure they derive from cenfure. At leaft it is no injuftice to conclude fo, where a perfon is extravagantly cenforious.

PERSONS of judgment and underftanding may be divided into two forts. Thofe whofe judgment is fo extenfive as to comprehend a great deal; exiftences, fyftems, univerfals : but as there

are

are some eyes so conftituted as to take in diftant
objects, yet be excelled by others in regard to
objects minute or near, so there are other underftandings better calculated for the examination
of particular objects.

The mind is at firft an open field without partitions or inclofures. To make it turn to moft
account, it is very proper to divide and inclofe;
in other words, to fort our obfervations.

Some men are called fagacious, merely on account of their avarice : whereas a child can clench
its fift the moment it is born.

It is a point of prudence, when you converfe
with your inferiour, to confider yourfelf as con-
verfing with his inferiour, with whom no doubt
he may have the fame connection that you have
with him ; and to be upon your guard accordingly.

How deplorable then is a perfon's condition,
when his mind can only be fupported by flattery,
and his conftitution but by cordials! when the
relief of his prefent complaint undermines its
own efficacy, yet increafes the occafion for which
it is ufed! Short is then the duration of our tranquillity, or of our lives!

A man is not efteemed ill-natured for any excefs of focial affection, or an indifcreet profu-
fion of his fortune upon his neighbours, companions, or friends ; although the true meafure of
his affections is as much impaired by this, as by
felfifhnefs.

If any one's curfe can effect damnation, it is
not that of the pope, but that of the poor. ·

People

PEOPLE of the fineſt and moſt lively genius have the greateſt ſenſibility, of conſequence the moſt lively paſſions; the violence of which puts their conduct upon a footing with that of fools. Fools diſcern the weakneſſes which they have in common with themſelves; but are not ſenſible of their excellencies to which they have no pretenſions; of courſe, always inclined to diſpute the ſuperiority.

WIT is the refractory pupil of judgment.

VIRTUE ſhould be conſidered as a part of taſte, (and perhaps it is ſo more in this age, than in any preceding one), and ſhould as much avoid deceit or ſiniſter meanings in diſcourſe, as they would do puns, bad language, or falſe grammar.

THINK when you are enraged at any one, what would probably become your ſentiments ſhould he die during the diſpute.

THE man of a towering ambition, or a well-regulated taſte, has fewer objects to envy or to covet than the grovellers.

REFINED ſenſe to a perſon that is to converſe alone with boors, is a manifeſt inconvenience. As Falſtaff ſays (with ſome little variation)

Company, witty company, has been the ruin of me.

IF envious people were univerſally to aſk themſelves, whether they would exchange their entire ſituations with the perſons envied, (I mean their minds, paſſions, notions, as well as their perſons, fortunes, dignities, &c. &c.), I will preſume

fume the felf-love common to human nature, would make them all prefer their own condition.

Quid ſtatis ? nolint — atqui licet eſſe beatis.

IF this rule were applied, as it ſurely ought to be, it bids fair to prove an univerſal cure for envy.

Quanto quiſque ſibi plura negaverit,
A diis plura feret. —— Self-denial.

A PERSON elevated one degree above the populace, aſſumes more airs of ſuperiority than one that is raiſed ten. The reaſon is ſomewhat obvious. His ſuperiority is more conteſtable·

THE character of a decent, well-behaved, gentleman-like man, ſeems more eaſily attainable by a perſon of no great parts or paſſions, than by one of greater genius and more volatility. It is there no miſmanagement, for the former to be chiefly ambitious of it.   When a man's capacity does not enable him to entertain or animate the company, it is the beſt he can do to render himſelf inoffenſive, and to keep his teeth clean. But the perſon who has talents for diſcourſe, and a paſſionate deſire to enliven converſation, ought to have many improprieties excuſed, which in the other were unpardonable. A lady of good-nature would forgive the blunder of a country-eſquire, who, through zeal to ſerve her with a glaſs of claret, ſhould involve his ſpurs in her

Bruſſels.

Bruffels apron. On the contrary, the fop (who may in fome fenfe ufe the words of Horace,

Quod verum atque decens curo et rogo, et
—— omnis in hoc fum)

would be entitled to no pardon for fuch unaccountable mifconduct.

MAN, in general, may be confidered as a mechanic, and the formation of happinefs as his bufinefs or employment ; virtue, his repofitory or collection of inftruments ; the goods of fortune as his materials : in proportion as the workman, the inftruments, and the materials excel, the work will be executed in the greater perfection.

THE filly cenforious are the very *fel naturae*, " the moft bitter of all bitter things ; " from the hyffop that grows upon the wall, to the fatirift that piffes againft it.

I HAVE known a fenfible man of opinion, that one fhould not be folicitous about a wife's underftanding. A woman's fenfe was with him a phrafe to exprefs a degree of knowledge, which was likely to contribute mighty little to a hufband's happinefs. I cannot be of his opinion. I am convinced, that as judgment is the portion of our fex, fo fancy and imagination are more eminently the lot of theirs. If fo, after honefty of heart, what is there we fhould fo much require ? A wife's beauty will foon decay, it is doubtful whether in reality firft, or in our own opinion. Either of thefe is fufficient to pall the

raptures

raptures of enjoyment. We are then to feek for fomething that will retain its novelty, or, what is equivalent, will change its fhape when her perfon palls by its identity. Fancy and genius bid faireft for this, which have as many fhapes as there can happen occafions to exert them. Good-nature I always fuppofe. The former will be expedient to exhilarate and divert us ; the latter to preferve our minds in a temper to be diverted.

I have known fome attorneys of reputable families, and whofe original difpofitions feemed to have been open and humane. Yet can I fcarce recollect one, in whom the gentleman, the Chriftian, and even the man, was not fwallowed up in the lawyer : they are not only the greateft tyrants, but the greateft pedants, of all mankind.

Reconciliation is the tendereft part either of friendfhip or of love ; the latter more efpecially, in which the foul is more remarkably foftened. Were a perfon to make ufe of art in procuring the affection of his miftrefs, it were, perhaps, his moft effectual method to contrive a flight eftrangement, and then, as it were imperceptibly, bring on a reconciliation. The foul here difcovers a kind of elafticity, and, being forced back, returns with an additional violence.

Virtue may be confidered as the only means of difpenfing happinefs in proper portions to every moment of our time.

To judge whether one has fufficient pleafure

to

to render the continuation of life agreeable, it is not enough to fay, Would you die ? Take away firft the hope of better fcenes in this life, the fears of worfe in another, and the bodily pain of dying.

THE fear of death feems as natural as the fenfation of luft or of hunger ; the firft and laft, for the prefervation of the individual ; the other, for the continuation of the fpecies.

. IT feems obvious, that God, who created the world, intends the happinefs and perfection of the fyftem he created. To effect the happinefs of the whole, felf love, in its degree, is as requifite as focial ; for I am myfelf a part of that whole, as well as another. The difficulty of afcertaining what is virtue, lies in proportioning the degrees of felf love and focial. *Proximus fum egomet mihi — Tunica pallio proprior.* — Charity begins at home. It is fo ; it ought to be fo ; nor is there any inconvenience arifes to the public, becaufe it is general. Were this away, the individual muft foon perifh, and confequently the whole body. A man has every moment occafion to exert his felf-love for the fake of felfprefervation ; confequently this ought to be ftronger, in order to keep him upon his guard. A centinel's attention fhould be greater than that of a foldier on a review.

THE focial, though alike conftant, is not equally intenfe, becaufe the felfifh, being univerfal, renders the focial lefs effential to the well-being of one's neighbour. In fhort, the felf love and

VOL. II.   Q   the

the focial ought to bear fuch proportion as we find they generally do. If the felfifh paffion of the reft preponderate, it would be felf-deftruc-tive in a few individuals to be over focially dif-pofed ; if the focial one prevails generally, to be of remarkable felfifhnefs muft obftruct the good of fociety.

MANY feel a fuperfluous uneafinefs for want of due attention to the following truth.

WE are oftentimes in fufpenfe betwixt the choice of different purfuits. We chufe one at laft doubtingly, and with an unconquered han-kering after the other. We find the fcheme which we have chofen anfwer our expectation but indifferently —— Moft worldly projects will. We, therefore, repent of our choice, and imme-diately fancy happinefs in the paths which we decline ; and this heightens our uneafinefs. We might at leaft efcape the aggravation of it. It is not improbable we had been more unhappy, but extremely probable we had not been lefs fo, had we made a different decifion. This, how-ever, relates to fchemes that are neither virtuous nor vitious.

HAPPY dogs (fays a certain fplenetic) our footmen and the populace ! Farewell, fays Æfop, in Vanbrugh, whom I both envy and defpife ! The fervant meets with hundreds whofe conver-fation can amufe him, for one that is the leaft qualified to be a companion for his mafter.

" A PERSON cannot eat his cake and have it," is, as Lord Shaftefbury obferves, a proper anfwer to many fplenetic people *. But what imports

* Complainants.

it

it to be in the poffeffion of a cake that you do not eat ? If then the cake be made to be eaten, fays Lady ——, better eat it, when you are moft hungry. Poor woman ! fhe feems to have act-ed by this maxim, but yet could not avoid cry-ing for the cake fhe had eaten.

You fhould calculate your appearance for the place where you refide. One would rather be a very knight in the country than his Honour Mr Such-a-one.

The moft confummate felfifhnefs would in-cline a perfon, at his death, to difpofe of his ef-fects agreeable to duty, that he may fecure an intereft in the world to which he is going.

A justice and his clerk is now little more than a blind man and his dog. The profound ignorance of the former, together with the ca-nine impudence and rapacity of the latter, will but rarely be found wanting to vindicate the com-parifon. The principal part of the fimilitude will appear obvious to every one ; I mean, that the juftice is as much dependent on his clerk, for fuperiour infight and implicit guidance, as the blind fellow on his cur that leads him in a ftring. Add to this, that the offer of a cruft will feduce the conductors of either to drag their mafters in-to a kennel.

To remark the different figure made by dif-ferent perfons under the fame circumftances of fortune ! Two friends of mine upon a journey had fo contrived as to reduce their finances to a fingle fixpence each. The one, with the genteel

and liberal air of abundance, gave his to a black
fhoe-boy, who wifhed his Honour a thoufand
bleffings; the other, having lodged a fortnight
with a nobleman that was his patron, offered his
to the butler, as an inftance of his gratitude, who
with difficulty forbore to curfe him to his face.

A GLASS or two of wine extraordinary, only
raifes a valetudinarian to that warmth of focial
affection, which had naturally been his lot in a
better ftate of health.

DEFERENCE is the moft complicate, the moft
indirect, and the moft elegant of all compliments.

BE cautious not to confider a perfon as your
fuperiour, merely becaufe he is your fuperiour
in point of affurance. This has often depreffed
the fpirit of a perfon of defert and diffidence.

A PROPER affurance, and competent fortune,
are effential to liberty.

TASTE is purfued at a lefs expenfe than fafhion.

OUR time in towns feems fhort to pafs, and
long to reflect upon; in the country, the reverfe.

DEFERENCE, before the company, is the gen-
teeleft kind of flattery. The flattery of epiftles
affects one lefs, as they cannot be fhewn without
an appearance of vanity. Flattery of the verbal kind is grofs. In fhort, applaufe is of too
coarfe a nature to be fwallowed in the grofs —
though the extract or tincture be ever fo agreeable.

WHEN a perfon, for a fplendid fervitude, fore-
goes an humble independency, it may be called
an advancement, if you pleafe: but it appears to
me

me an advancement from the pit to the gallery. Liberty is a more invigorating cordial than tokay.

THOUGH punctilios are trifling, they may be as important as the friendships of some persons that regard them — Indeed it is almost an universal practice to rail at punctilio ; and it seems in some measure a consequence of our attachment to French fashions. However, it is extremely obvious, that punctilio never caused half the quarrels that have risen from the freedom of behaviour, which is its opposite extreme. Were all men rational and civilized, the use of ceremony would be superfluous : but as the case is, it at least fixes some bounds to the encroachments of eccentric people, who, under the denomination of freedom, might demand the privilege of breaking your head.

THERE seem near as many people that want passion as want reason.

THE world would be more happy, if persons gave up more time to an intercourse of friendship. But money ingrosses all our deference ; and we scarce enjoy a social hour, because we think it unjustly stolen from the main business of our lives.

THE state of man is not unlike that of a fish hooked by an angler. Death allows us a little line. We flounce, and sport, and vary our situation : but when we would extend our schemes, we discover our confinement, checked and limited by a superiour hand, who drags us from our element whensoever he pleases.

THE vulgar trace your faults, those you have

Q 3 - - in

in common with themfelves; but they have no idea of your excellencies, to which they have no pretenfions.

A PERSON is fomething taller by holding up his head.

A MAN of fenfe can be adequately efteemed by none other than a man of fenfe; a fool by none but a fool. We ought to act upon this principle.

How melancholy is it to travel late and fatigued, upon any ambitious project, on a winter's night; and obferve the lights of cottages, where all the unambitious people are warm, and happy, or at reft in their beds; fome of them, fays W——, as wretched as princes, for aught we know to the contrary!

IT is generally a principle of indolence that makes one fo difgufted with an artful character. We hate the confinement of ftanding centinels in our own defence.

To behave with complaifance, where one forefees one muft needs quarrel, is like eating before a vomit.

SOME perfons may with juftice boaft, that they knew as much as others when they were but ten years old; and that their prefent knowledge comprehends after the manner that a larger trunk contains the fmaller ones it inclofes.

IT is poffible to difcover in fome faces the features nature intended, had fhe not been fomehow thwarted in her operations. Is it not eafy to remark the fame diftortion in fome minds? There is a phrafe pretty frequent amongft the vulgar,

vulgar, and which they apply to abfolute fools,
—That they have had a rock too much in their
cradles.—With me, it is a moft expreffive idiom
to defcribe a diflocated underftanding ; an underftanding, for inftance, which, like a watch,
difcovers a multitude of fuch parts as appear
obvioufly intended to belong to a fyftem of the
greateft perfection, yet which, by fome unlucky
jumble, falls infinitely fhort of it.

Is it not the wound our pride fuftains by being
deceived, that makes us more averfe to hypocrites
than to the moft audacious and barefaced villain ? Yet it feems as much a piece of juftice to
commend a man for talking more honeftly than
he acts, as it is to blame a man for acting more
difhoneftly than he talks. The fum of the
whole, however, is, that the one adds to other
crimes by his deceit, and the other by his impudence.

A FOOL can neither eat, nor drink, nor ftand,
nor walk, nor, in fhort, laugh nor cry, nor take
fnuff, like a man of fenfe. How obvious the
diftinction !. Independency may be found in comparative as well as abfolute abundance ; I mean
where a perfon contracts his defires within the
limits of his fortune.

THERE are very few perfons who do not lofe
fomething of their efteem for you, upon your
approach to familiarity.

THE filly excufe that is often drawn from want
of time to correfpond, becomes no one befide a
cobler with ten or a dozen children dependent on
a tatching end.

ONE.

ONE, perhaps, ought to make funerals as sumptuous as possible, or as private ; either by obscurity to elude, or by splendour to employ, the attention, that it may not be engaged by the most shocking circumstance of our humanity.

IT happens a little unluckily, that the persons who have the most intimate contempt of money, are the same that have the strongest appetites for the pleasures it procures.

WE are apt to look for those virtues in the characters of noblemen, that are but rarely to be found any where, except in the preambles to their patents. Some shining exceptions may be made to this rule : In general we may consider their appearance with us in public, as one does our wearing apparel. " Which lord do you wear " to-day ? Why, I did think to wear my Lord " ****; but as there will be little company in the " Mall, I will e'en content myself to wear the " same noble peer I wore yesterday."

THE worst inconvenience of a small fortune is, that it will not admit of inadvertency. Inadvertency, however, ought to be placed at the head of most mens yearly accounts, and a sum as regularly allotted to it as to any other article.

IT is with our judgments, as with our eyes. Some can see objects at a greater distance more distinctly, at the same time less distinctly than others the objects that are near them.

NOTWITHSTANDING the airs men give themselves, I believe no one sees family to more advantage than the persons that have no share in it.

How

How important is the eye to the appearance of an human face! the chief index of temper, underftanding, health, and love. What prodigious influence muft the fame misfortunes have on fome perfons beyond others! as the lofs of an eye to a mere infolent beauty, without the leaft philofophy to fupport herfelf!

The perfon leaft referved in his abufe of another's excefs in equipage, is commonly the perfon who would exhibit the fame if it had been within his power; the fource of both being a difregard to decorum. Likewife he that violently arraigns, or fondly indulges it, agree in confidering it a little too ferioufly.

Amid the moft mercenary ages, it is but a fecondary fort of admiration that is beftowed upon magnificence.

An order of beauties, as of knights, with a ftyle appropriated to them, (as for inftance, To the Right Beautiful Lady Such-a-one), would have as good a foundation as any other clafs, but would, at the fame time, be the moft invidious of any order that was ever inftituted.

The firft maxim a child is taught, is, that

Learning is better than houfe and land;

but how little is its influence as he grows up to maturity!

There is fomewhat very aftonifhing in the record of our moft celebrated victories: I mean the fmall number of the conquerors killed in proportion to the conquered. At Agincourt, it is faid, were ten thoufand, and fourteen thoufand maffacred.

maffacred. Livy's accounts of this fort are fo
aftonifhing, that one is apt to difbelieve the hiftorian.—All the explanation one can find, is,
that the grofs flaughter is made when one fide
takes to flight.

A person that is difpofed to throw off all
referve before an inferiour, fhould reflect, that
he has alfo his inferiours to whom he may be
equally communicative.

It is impoffible for a man of fenfe to guard
againft the mortification that may be given him
by fools, or heteroclite characters, becaufe he
cannot forefee them. A wit-would cannot afford
to difcard a frivolous conceit, though it tends to
affront you : An old maid, a country-put, or a
college-pedant, will ignorantly or wilfully blunder
upon fuch hints as muft difcompofe you.

A man that is folicitous about his health, or
apprehenfive of fome acute diforder, fhould write
a journal of his conftitution for the better in-
ftruction of his phyfician.

Ghosts have no more connection with darknefs, than the miftery of a barber with that of
a furgeon; yet we find they go together. Perhaps Nox and Chaos were their mythological
parents.

He makes a lady but a poor recompenfe who
marries her, becaufe he has kept her company
long after his affection is eftranged. Does he
not rather increafe the injury ?

Second thoughts oftentimes are the very worft
of all thoughts. Firft and third very often coincide. Indeed fecond thoughts are too frequently

quently formed by the love of novelty, of fhewing penetration, of diftinguifhing ourfelves from
the mob, and have confequently lefs of fimplicity, and more of affectation. This, however,
regards principally objects of tafte and fancy.
Third thoughts, at leaft, are here very proper
mediators.

" SET a beggar on horfe-back, and he'll ride,"
is a common proverb and a real truth. The
novus homo is an *inexpertus homo*, and confequently muft purchafe finery, before he knows the
emptinefs of it experimentally. The eftablifhed
gentleman difregards it through habit and familiarity.

THE foppery of love-verfes, when a perfon is
ill and indifpofed, is perfect ipecacuanha.

ANTIQUITY of family, and diftinctions of
gentry, have, perhaps, lefs weight in this age
than they had ever heretofore. The bend dex-
ter or finifter, the chief, the canton, or the che-
veron, are greatly out of date. The heralds are
at length difcovered to have no legal authority.
Spain, indeed, continues to preferve the diftinction, and is poor. France (by our difpute about
a trading nobility) feems inclined to fhake it off.
Who now looks with veneration on the antedi-
luvian pedigree of a Welchman? Property either
is, or is fure to purchafe, diftinction, let the king
at arms, or the old maiden aunt preach as long
as either pleafes. It is fo; perhaps it ought to
be fo. All honours fhould lie open, all encouragement be allowed to the members of trade in

a

a trading nation : And as the nobility find it
very expedient to partake of their profits, fo
they, in return, fhould obtain a fhare in the others
honours.   One would, however, wifh the acquifition of learning was as fure a road to dignity
as that of riches.

On

ON BOOKS AND WRITERS.

IT is often afferted by pretenders to fingular penetration, that the affiftance fancy is fuppofed to draw from wine is merely imaginary and chimerical: that all which the poets have urged on this head is abfolute rant and enthufiafm, and has no foundation in truth or nature. I am inclined to think otherwife. Judgment; I readily allow, derives no benefit from the nobleft cordial. But perfons of a phlegmatic conftitution have thofe excellencies often fuppreffed, of which their imagination is truly capable; by reafon of a lentor, which wine may naturally remove. It raifes low fpirits to a pitch neceffary for the exertion of fancy. It confutes the *Non eſt tanti*, fo frequently a maxim with fpeculative perfons. It quickens that ambition, or that focial bias, which makes a perfon wifh to fhine, or to pleafe. Afk what tradition fays of Mr Addifon's converfation. But inftances in point of converfation come within every one's obfervance. Why then may it not be allowed to produce the fame effects in writing?

THE affected phrafes I hate moft, are thofe on which your half-wits found their reputation; fuch as *pretty trifler*, *fair plaintiff*, *lovely architect*, &c.

DOCTOR YOUNG has a furprifing knack of bringing thoughts from a diftance from their lurking-places, in a moment's time.

THERE is nothing fo difagreeable in works of

humour as an infipid, unfupported vivacity; the very hufks of drollery; bottled fmall-beer; a man outriding his horfe; lewdnefs and impotence; a fiery actor in a phlegmatic fcene; an illiterate and ftupid preacher difcourfing upon Urim and Thummim, and beating the pulpit-cufhion in fuch manner as though he would make the duft and the truth fly out of it at once.

An editor, or a tranflator, collects the merits of different writers; and, forming all into a wreath, beftows it on his author's tomb. The thunder of Demofthenes, the weight of Tully, the judgment of Tacitus, the elegance of Livy, the fublimity of Homer, the majefty of Virgil, the wit of Ovid, the propriety of Horace, the accuracy of Terence, the brevity of Phædrus, and the poignancy of Juvenal, (with every name of note he can poffibly recall to mind), are given to fome ancient fcribbler, in whom affectation and the love of novelty difpofes him to find out beauties.

HUMOUR and Vanbrugh againft Wit and Congreve.

THE vacant fcull of a pedant generally furnifhes out a throne and a temple for vanity.

MAY not the cuftom of fcraping when we bow, be derived from the ancient cuftom of throwing their fhoes backward off their feet?

" A BIRD in the air fhall carry the tale, and " that which hath wings fhall tell the matter." Such is alfo the prefent phrafe — " A little bird " told it me,"——fays nurfe ——

The preference which fome give to Virgil before Homer, is often owing to complexion. Some are more formed to enjoy the grand; and others, the beautiful. But as for invention and fublimity, the moft fhining qualities of imagination, there is furely no comparifon between them.—Yet I enjoy Virgil more.

Agreeable ideas rife in proportion as they are drawn from inanimates, from vegetables, from animals, and from human creatures.

One reafon why the found is fometimes an echo to the fenfe, is, that the pleafanteft objects have often the moft harmonious names annexed to them.

A man of a merely argumentative caft, will read poetry as profe; will only regard the quantum it contains of folid reafoning: juft as a clown attacks a deffert, confidering it as fo much victuals; and regardlefs of thofe lively or emblematical decorations which the cook, for many fleeplefs nights, has endeavoured to beftow upon it.

Notwithstanding all that Roufleau has advanced fo very ingeniously upon plays and players, their profeffion is, like that of a painter, one of the imitative arts, whofe means are pleafure, and whofe end is virtue. They both alike, for a fubfiftence, fubmit themfelves to public opinion; and the difhonour that has attended the laft profeffion, feems not eafily accountable.

As there are evidently words in Englifh poetry that have all the force of a dactyl, and, if properly inferted, have no fmall beauty on that ac-

count,

count, it feems abfurd to contract or print them
otherwife than at length.

The loofe wall tottering o'er the trembling fhade:
       OGILVY's Day of Judgment.

Trembling has alfo the force of a dactyl in a
lefs degree—but cannot be written otherwife.

I HAVE fometimes thought Virgil fo remarkably mufical, that were his lines read to a mufician
wholly ignorant of the language, by a perfon of
capacity to give each word its proper accent, he
would not fail to diftinguifh in it all the graces of
harmony.

I THINK I can obferve a peculiar beauty in
the addition of a fhort fyllable, at the end of a
blank verfe : I mean, however, in blank dialogue:
In other poetry it is as fure to flatten : which
may be difcerned in Prior's tranflation of Calli-
machus, *viz.* — *the holy victim* — *Dictæan hear'ft*
thou — — *birth, great Rhea* — — *inferiour reptile* — ''
&c. &c. for the tranflation abounds with them;
and is rendered by that means profaic.

THE cafe is only, profe being an imitation of
common life, the nature of an ode requires that
it fhould be lifted fome degrees higher.

BUT in dialogue, the language ought never
to leave nature the leaft out of fight, and efpecially, where pity is to be produced, it appears to
receive an advantage from the melancholy flow
this fyllable occafions. Let me produce a few
inftances from Otway's tragedy of the Unhappy
Marriage; and, in order to form a judgment, let
                                    the

the reader fubftitute a word of equal import,
but of a fyllable lefs, in the place of the inftances I produce. (Some inftances are numberlefs, where they familiarize and give an eafe to
dialogue.)

——*Sure my ill fates upon mĕ.*

—*Why was I not laid in my peaceful grave,*
    With my poor parents, and at reft as they ăre?

—*I never fee you now—you have been kindĕr.*

—*Why was I made with all my fex's foftnĕfs,*
  . *Yet want the cunning to conceal its folliĕs?*
    I'll fee Caftalio—tax him with his falfehood?

            ——*Should you charge rough,*
  I fhould but weep, and anfwer you with fobbing.

—*When thou art from me, every place is desĕrt.*

            ——*Surely Paradife is round me,*
And every fenfe is full of thy perfection.
To hear thee fpeak might calm a madman's frenzy,
Till, by attention, he forgot his forrows.

—*'Till good men wifh him dead—or I offend him.*

—*And hang upon you, like a drowning creature.*

—*Cropt this fair rofe, and rifled all its fweetnefs.*

—*Give me Chamont, and let the world forfake me.*

            ——*I've drank an healing draught*
For all my cares, and never more fhall wrong thee.

—*When I'm laid low in the cold grave forgotten,*
  May you be happy in a fairer bride,
    But none can ever love you, like Monimia.

R 3   L

I should imagine, that, in some or most of these examples, a particular degree of tenderness is owing to the supernumerary syllable; yet it requires a nice ear for the disposition of it, (for it must not be universal); and, with this, may give at once an harmonious flow, a natural ease, an energy, tenderness, and variety to the language.

A MAN of dry sound judgment attends to the truth of a proposition;——a man of ear, and sensibility, to the music of the versification : a man of a well-regulated taste, finds the former more deeply imprinted on him, by the judicious management of the latter.

It seems to me that what are called notes at the bottom of pages (as well as parentheses in writing) might be generally avoided, without injuring the thread of a discourse. It is true it might require some address to interweave them gracefully into the text; but how much more agreeable would be the effect, than to interrupt the reader by such frequent avocations? How much more graceful to play a tune upon one set of keys, with varied stops, than to seek the same variety, by an awkward motion from one set to another ?

It bears a little hard upon our candour, that *to take to pieces* in our language signifies the same as *to expose;* and *to expose* has a signification, which good-nature can as little allow, as can the laws of etymology.

THE ordinary letters from friend to friend seem capable of receiving a better turn than
mere

merc compliment, frivolous intelligence, or pro-
feffions of friendfhip continually repeated. The
eftablifhed maxim to correfpond with eafe, has
almoft excluded every ufeful fubject: but may
not excefs of negligence difcover affectation, as
well as its oppofite extreme? There are many
degrees of intermediate folidity betwixt a Weft-
phalia ham and a whip fyllabub.

I am aftonifhed to remark the defect of ear
which fome tolerably harmonious poets difcover
in their alexandrines. It feems wonderful that
an errour fo obvious, and fo very difguftful to a
nice ear, fhould occur fo frequently as the following:

What feraph e'er could preach
So choice a lecture as his wondrous virtue's lore?

The paufe being after the fixth fyllable, it is
plain the whole emphafis of pronunciation is
thrown upon the particle *as*. It feems moft a-
mazing to me, that this fhould be fo common a
blunder.

Simplex munditiis has been efteemed univerfally to be a phrafe at once very expreffive, and
of very difficult interpretation; at leaft, not very
capable to be explained without circumlocution.
What objection can we make to that fingle word,
elegant? which excludes the glare and multipli-
city of ornaments on one fide, as much as it
does dirt and rufticity on the other.

The French ufe the word *naive* in fuch a
fenfe as to be explainable by no Englifh word;
unlefs

unlefs we will fubmit to reftrain ourfelves in the application of the word *fentimental*. It means the language of paffion, or the heart; in oppofition to the language of reflection, and the head.

THE moft frequent miftake that is made, feems to be that of the means for the end: thus riches for happinefs, and thus learning for fenfe. The former of thefe is hourly obfervable: and as to the latter, methinks this age affords frequent and furprifing inftances.

IT is with real concern, that I obferve many perfons of true poetical genius endeavouring to quench their native fire, that they may exhibit learning without a fingle fpark of it. Nor is it uncommon to fee an author tranflate a book, when with half the pains he could write a better; but the tranflation favours more of learning, and gives room for notes, which exhibit more.

LEARNING, like money, may be of fo bafe a coin, as to be utterly void of ufe; or, if fterling, may require good management, to make it ferve the purpofes of fenfe or happinefs.

WHEN a nobleman has once conferred any great favour on his inferiour, he ought thenceforth to confider that his requefts, his advice, and even his intimations become commands; and to propofe matters with the utmoft tendernefs. The perfon whom he obliges has otherwife loft his freedom.

Hac ego fi compellar imagine, cuncta refigno:
Nec fomnum plebis laudo fatur altilium; nec
Otia divitiis Arabum liberrima muto.

THE

THE amiable and the fevere, Mr Burke's fublime and beautiful, by different proportions are mixed in every character. Accordingly as either is predominant, men imprint the paffions of love or fear. The beft punch depends on a proper mixture of fugar and lemon.

THERE are many perfons acquire to them-felves a character of infincerity, from what is in truth mere inconftancy. And there are perfons of warm, but changeable paffions, per-haps the fincereft of any in the very inftant they make profeffion, but the very leaft to be de-pended on through the fhort duration of all ex-tremes. It has often puzzled me, on this ac-count, to afcertain the character of Lady Lux-borough; yet whatever were her principles, I e-fteem Lord Bolingbroke's to have been the fame. She feemed in all refpects the female Lord Bo-lingbroke.

THE principal, if not the only, difference be-twixt honefty and honour, feems to lie in their different motives; the object of the latter be-ing reputation, and of the former duty.

IT is the greateft comfort to the poor, whofe ignorance often inclines them to an ill-grounded envy, that the rich muft die as well as themfelves.

THE common people call wit, mirth; and fancy, folly; fanciful and folliful they ufe in-difcriminately. It feems to flow from hence, that they confider money as of more importance than the perfons who poffefs it, and that no conduct is wife befide what has a tendency to enrich us.

ONE fhould not deftroy an infect, one fhould not quarrel with a dog, without a reafon fufficient

ficient to vindicate one through all the courts of morality.

THE trouble occasioned by want of a servant, is so much less than the plague of a bad one, as it is less painful to clean a pair of shoes than undergo an excess of anger.

THE fund of sensible discourse is limited; that of jest and badinerie is infinite. In many companies then, where nothing is to be learned, it were, perhaps, better to get upon the familiar footing; to give and take in the way of raillery.

WHEN a wife or mistress lives as in a jail, the person that confines her lives the life of a jailor.

THERE seems some analogy betwixt a person's manner in every action of his life.

LADY Luxborough's hand-writing was, at the same time, delicate and masculine. Her features, her air, her understanding, her motions, and her sentiments, were the same. Mr W——, in the same respects, delicate, but not masculine. Mr G——— rather more delicate than masculine. Mr J——— rather more masculine than delicate. And this, in regard to the three last, extends to their drawing, versification, &c. &c. &c.

RICHES deserve the attention of young persons rather than old ones, though the practice is otherwise.

To consume one's time and fortune at once, without pleasure, recompense, or figure, is like pouring forth one's spirits rather in phlebotomy than enjoyment.

PARENTS

PARENTS are generally partial to great vivacity in their children, and are apt to be more or lefs fond of them in proportion to it. Perhaps there cannot be a fymptom lefs expreffive of future judgment and folidity. It feems thoroughly to preclude not only depth of penetration, but alfo delicacy of fentiment. Neither does it feem any way confiftent with a fenfibility of pleafure, notwithftanding all external appearances. It is a mere greyhound puppy in a warren, that runs at all truths, and at all forts of pleafure; but does not allow itfelf time to be fuccefsful in fecuring any. It is a bufy bee, whofe whole time paffes away in mere flight from flower to flower, without refting upon any a fufficient time to gather honey.

THE Queen of Sweden declared, " fhe did not " love men as men, but merely becaufe they " were not women." What a fpirited piece of fatire !

IN mixed converfation, or amongft perfons of no great knowledge, one indulges one's felf in difcourfe that is neither ingenious nor fignificant. Vapid frivolous chit-chat ferves to pafs away the time. But corked up again in retirement, we recover our wonted ftrength, fpirit, and flavour.

THE making prefents to a lady one addreffes, is like throwing armour into an enemy's camp, with a refolution to recover it.

HE that lies abed all a fummer's morning, lofes the chief pleafure of the day: he that gives up his youth to indolence, undergoes a lofs of the fame kind.

SPLEEN

SPLEEN is often little elfe than obftructed per-
fpiration.

THE regard men externally profefs for their
fuperiours, is oftentimes rewarded — in the manner it deferves.

METHINKS all men fhould meet with a refpect
due to as high a character as they can act be-
comingly.

SHINING characters are not always the moft
agreeable ones. The mild radiance of an eme-
rald is by no means lefs pleafing than the glare
of a ruby.

MANKIND fuffers more by the conflict of contrary paffions, than that of paffion and reafon :
yet, perhaps, the trueft way to quench one paffion is to kindle up another.

PRUDENT men fhould lock up their motives,
giving only their intimates a key.

THE country-efquire limits his ambition to a
pre-eminence in the knowledge of horfes ; that
is, of an animal that may convey him with eafe,
credit, and fafety, the little journeys he has to
go. The philofopher directs his ambition to
fome well-grounded fcience, which may, with
the fame credit, eafe, and fafety, tranfport him
through every ftage of being ; fo that he may
not be overthrown by paffion, nor trailed infi-
pidly along by apathy.

TOM Tweedle played a good fiddle ; but, nothing fatisfied with the inconfiderable appellation
of a fiddler, dropped the practice, and is now no
character.

THE beft time to frame an anfwer to the

letters of a friend, is the moment you receive them. Then the warmth of friendſhip, and the intelligence received, moſt forcibly co-operate.

THE philoſophers and ancient ſages, who declaimed againſt the vanity of all external advantages, ſeem in an equal degree to have countenanced and authoriſed the mental ones, or they would condemn their own example.

SUPERIORITY in wit is more frequently the cauſe of vanity than ſuperiority of judgment ; as the perſon that wears an ornamental ſword, is ever more vain than he that wears an uſeful one.

THE perſon who has a ſuperiority in wit, is enabled, by the means of it, to ſee his ſuperiority : hence a deference expected, and offence taken, upon the failure. Add to this, that wit, conſidered as fancy, renders all the paſſions more ſenſible ; the love of fame more remarkably ſo ; and you have ſome ſort of reaſon for the revenge taken by wits upon thoſe who neglect them.

IN the quarrels of our friends, it is incumbent on us to take a part ;—in the quarrels of mere acquaintance, it is needleſs, and perhaps impertinent.

WHEN I have purchaſed aught by way of mere amuſement, your reflection upon the coſt not only intimates the bargain I have made to be a bad one, but tends to make it ſo.

" HAD I the money thoſe paintings coſt," ſays Torpor, " methinks I would have diſcovered " ſome better method of diſpoſing of it." " And " in what would you have expended it ?" " I
" would

" would buy fome fine horfes." " But you have
" already what anfwer your purpofe !" " Yes,
" but I have a particular fancy for a fine horfe."
" And have not I, who bought thefe pictures,
" the fame argument on my fide ?"   The truth
is, he who extols his own amufements, and condemns another perfon's, unlefs he does it as they
bear relation to virtue or vice, will at all times
find himfelf at a lofs for an argument.

PEOPLE of real genius have ftrong paffions ;
people of ftrong paffions have great partiali-
ties ; fuch as Mr Pope for Lord Bolingbroke,
&c. Perfons of flow parts have languid paffions,
and perfons of languid paffions have little partiality. They neither love, nor hate, nor look,
nor move, with the energy of a man of fenfe.
The faults of the former fhould be balanced
with their excellencies ; and the blamelefluefs of
the latter fhould be weighed with their infigni-
ficancy. Happinefs and virtue are, perhaps, generally difpenfed with more equality than we are
aware.

EXTREME volatile and fprightly tempers feem
inconfiftent with any great enjoyment. There
is too much time wafted in the mere tranfition
from one object to another. No room for thofe
deep impreffions which are made alone by the
duration of an idea ; and are quite requifite to
any ftrong fenfation either of pleafure or of
pain.. The bee to collect honey, or the fpider
to gather poifon, muft abide fome time upon
the weed or flower. They whofe fluids are mere
fal volatile, feem rather cheerful than happy men.

S 2   The

The temper above defcribed is oftener the lot of wits than of perfons of great abilities.

THERE are no perfons more folicitous about the prefervation of rank than thofe who have no rank at all. Obferve the humours of a country-chriftening, and you will find no court in Chriftendom fo ceremonious as the quality of Brentford.

CRITICS will fometimes prefer the faulty ftate of a compofition to the improved one, through mere perverfenefs: in like manner fome will extol a perfon's paft conduct, to depretiate his prefent. Thefe are fome of the numerous fhifts and machinations of envy.

TREES afford us the advantage of fhade in fummer, as well as fuel in winter; as the fame virtue allays the fervour of intemperate paffions in our youth, and ferves to comfort and keep us warm amid the rigours of old age.

THE term *indecifion*, in a man's character, implies an idea very nicely different from that of irrefolution; yet it has a tendency to produce it; and, like that, has often its original in exceffive delicacy and refinement.

PERSONS of proud yet abject fpirits will defpife you for thofe diftreffes for which the generous mind will pity, and endeavour to befriend you: A hint, to whom only you fhould difclofe, and from whom you fhould conceal them. Yet, perhaps, in general, it may be prudent to conceal them from perfons of an oppofite party.

THE facrificing of our anger to our intereft is

oftentimes

oftentimes no more than the exchange of a painful paffion for a pleafurable.

There are not five in five hundred that pity, but at the fame time alfo defpife; a reafon that you fhould be cautious to whom and where you complain. The furtheft a prudent man fhould proceed, in general, is to laugh at fome of his own foibles, when this may be a means of removing envy from the more important parts of his character.

Effeminacy of appearance, and an exceffive attention to the minuter parts of drefs, is, I believe, properly, in the general run, efteemed a fymptom of irrefolution. But yet inftances are feen to abound in the French nation to the contrary. And in our own, that of Lord Mark Kerr was an inftance equal to a thoufand. A fnuff-box hinge rendered invifible, was an object on which his happinefs appeared to turn; which, however, might be clouded by a fpeck of dirt, or wounded by a hole in the heel of his ftocking. Yet this man's intrepidity was fhewn beyond all contradiction. What fhall we fay then of Mr ——, of manners very delicate, yet poffeffed of a poetical vein fraught with the nobleft and fublimeft images, and of a mind remarkably well ftored with the more mafculine parts of learning?—Here, perhaps, we muft remain in fufpenfe;—for though tafte does not imply manners, fo neither does it preclude them: or what hinders, that a man fhould feel that fame delicacy in regard to real honour, which he does in regard to drefs?

If

IF beneficence be not in a perfon's will, what imports it to mankind, that it is ever fo much in his power? And yet we fee how much more regard is generally paid to a worthlefs man of fortune, than to the moft benevolent beggar that ever uttered an ineffectual bleffing. It is all agreeable to Mr Burke's thefis, that the formidable idea of power affects more deeply than the moft beautiful image we can conceive of moral virtue.

A PERSON that is not merely ftupid, is naturally under the influence of the acute paflions, or the flow. — The principle of revenge is meant for the fecurity of the individual; and fuppofing a perfon his not courage to put it immediately into practice, he commonly ftrives to make himfelf remarkable for the perfeverance of his refentment. Both thefe have the fame motive to imprefs a dread upon our enemies of injuring us for the future: and though the world be more inclined to favour the rafh than the phlegmatic enemy, it is hard to fay which of the two has given rife to more difmal confequences.—The reafon of this partiality may be deduced from the fame original, as the preference that is given to downright impudence before hypocrify. To be cheated into an ill-placed efteem, or to be undermined by concealed malignity, difcovers a contempt for our underftanding, and leffens the idea we entertain of it ourfelves. They hurt our pride more than open violence, or undifguifed impudence.

KING James the Firft, willing to involve the regal power in myftery, that like natural objects

it

it might appear greater through the fog, declared it prefumption for a fubject to fay, " what " a king might do in the fulnefs of his power."
——This was abfurd; but it feems prefumption in a man of the world, to fay what means a man of genius may think inftrumental to his happinefs. W—— ufed to fay, it was prefumption for him to make conjectures on the occafion. A perfon of refinement feems to have his pleafures diftinct from the common run of men; what the world calls important, is to him wholly frivolous; and what the world efteems frivolous, feems effential to his tranquillity.

THE apparatus of a funeral among the middle rank of people, and fometimes among the great, has one effect that is not frivolous. It in fome meafure diffipates and draws off the attention from the main object of concern. Weaker minds find a fort of relief in being compelled to give directions about the manner of interment: and the grave folemnity of the hearfe, plumes, and efcutcheons, though they add to the force of terrour, diminifh that of fimple grief.

THERE are fome people whom you cannot regard, though they feem defirous to oblige you, nay, even though they do you actual fervices. This is the cafe where-ever their fentiments are too widely different from your own. Thus a perfon truly avaricious can never make himfelf truly agreeable to one enamoured with the arts and fciences. A perfon of exquifite fenfibility and tendernefs can never be truly pleafed with another of no feelings; who can fee the moft
intimate

intimate of his friends or kindred expire without any greater pain than if he beheld a pitcher broken. Thefe, properly fpeaking, can be faid to feel nothing but the point of a fword; and one could more eafily pardon them, if this apathy were the effect of philofophy, and not want of thought. But what I would inculcate, is, with tempers thus different one fhould never attempt any clofe connection.

Lupis et agnis quanta fortito obtigit,
Tecum mihi difcordia eft.

Yet it may be a point of prudence to fhew them civility, and allow a toleration to their various propenfities. To converfe much with them, would not only be painful, but tend to injure your own difpofition; and to aim at obtaining their applaufe, would only make your character inconfiftent.

There are fome people who find a gloomy kind of pleafure in glouting, which could hardly be increafed by the fatisfaction of having their wifhes granted. This is, feemingly, a bad character, and yet often connected with a fenfe of honour, of confcious merit, with warm gratitude, great fincerity, and many other valuable qualities.

There is a degree of underftanding in women with which one not only ought to be contented, but abfolutely pleafed.——One would not in them require the unfathomable abyfs.

The worft confequence of gratifying our paffions in regard to objects of an indifferent nature,

ture, is, that it caufes them to proceed with greater violence towards other and other objects, and fo *ad infinitum*. I wifh, for my pocket, an elegant *etui*; and gold to remove the pain of wifhing, and partake the pleafure of enjoyment. I would part with the purchafe-money, for which I have lefs regard; but the gratification of this wifh would generate fifty others, that would be ruinous. See Epictetus; who, therefore, advifes to refift the firft.

VIRTUE and agreeablenefs are, I fear, too often feparated; that is, externals affect and captivate the fancy, where internal worth is wanting to engage and attach one's reafon :--- A moft perplexing circumftance; and no where more remarkable, than when we fee a wife man totally enflaved by the beauty of a perfon he defpifes.

I KNOW not whether increafing years do not caufe one to efteem fewer people, and to bear with more.

QUERE, whether friendfhip for the fex do not tend to leffen the fenfual appetite, and *vice verfa ?*

I THINK I never knew an inftance of great quicknefs of parts being joined with great folidity. The moft rapid rivers are feldom or never deep.

To be at once a rake, and to glory in the character, difcovers at the fame time a bad difpofition and a bad tafte.

THERE are perfons who flide infenfibly into an habit of contradiction. Their firft endeavour, upon hearing aught afferted, is to difcover where-

in.

in it may be plaufibly difputed. This, they imagine, gives an air of great fagacity; and if they
can mingle a jeft with contradiction, think they
difplay great fuperiority. One fhould be cautious
againft the advances of this kind of propenfity,
which lofes us friends, in a matter generally of
no confequence.

The folicitude of peers to preferve or to ex-
alt their rank, is efteemed no other than a
manly and becoming ambition. The care of commoners on the fame fubject is deemed either vanity, formality, or pride.

An income for life only feems the beft calculated for the circumftances and fituation of mortal man : the farther property in an eftate increafes the difficulty of difengaging our affections
from this world, and of thinking in the manner
we ought to think of a fyftem from which we
muft be entirely feparated.

I truft that finking fund, my life.

POPE.

Surprise quickens enjoyment, and expectation banifhes furprife. This is the fimple reafon
why few pleafures that have ingroffed our attention previoufly, ever anfwer our ideas of them.
Add to this, that imagination is a great magnifier, and caufes the hopes we conceive to grow
too large for their object.---Thus expectation does
not only deftroy the advantage of furprife, and
fo flattens pleafure ; but makes us hope for an
imaginary addition, which gives the pain of difappointment.

On

On RELIGION.

IF people were to bawl out, " God for ever !
" Huzza !" (which is a mark of refpect to
kings upon any event that is deferving of national gratitude),why were not this equivalent to
a regular thankfgiving ? At leaft zealots and de ·
votees, who are fuch mighty advocates for the
fervour of devotion, fhould prefer it, as what is
generally more fincere and unaffected.

II.

Perhaps we fhould not pray to God " to
" keep us ftedfaft in any faith," but condition-
ally, that it be a right one.

III.

When a tree is falling, I have feen the labour-
ers, by a trivial jerk with a rope, throw it upon
the fpot where they would wifh it fhould lie. Divines underftanding this text too literally, pretend, by a little interpofition in the article of
death, to regulate a perfon's everlafting happinefs. I fancy the allufion will hardly countenance their prefumption.

When misfortunes happen to fuch as diffent
from us in matters of religion, we call them judgments ; when to thofe of our own fect, we call
them trials ; when to perfons neither way diftinguifhed, we are content to impute them to the
fettled courfe of things.

In regard to church-mufic, if a man cannot
be faid to be merry or good-humoured when he
is

is tickled till he laughs, why fhould he be efteemed devout or pious, when he is tweedled into zeal
by the dron pipe of an organ?—In anfwer to
this it may be faid, that if fuch an elevation of
the fpirits be not meritorious, be not devotion,
yet it is attended with good confequences ; as it
leaves a good impreffion upon the mind, favourable to virtue and a religious life.

THE rich man, adjoining to his country-feat,
erects a chapel, as he pretends, to God Almighty,
but, in truth, to his own vain-glory ; furnifhes it
with luxurious conveniencies for prayers that
will be never faid. The poor man kneels by his
bed-fide, and goes to heaven before him.

I SHOULD think a clergyman might diftinguifh
himfelf by compofing a fet of fermons upon the
ordinary virtues extolled in claffic writers, introducing the ornamental flourifhes of Horace, Juvenal, &c.

1. AGAINST family-pride might be taken from
Juvenal's *Stemmata quid faciunt*, Horace's *Non
quia Moecenas*, and Marius's fpeech in Salluft.
The text, " Is not this Jofeph the carpenter's fon?"

2. A SERMON upon the advantages of com-
petency, contentment, and rural life, might be
abundantly embellifhed from the claffics, and
would be both grateful and ferviceable to the
common people; as the chief paffion from which
they fuffer is envy, I believe, mifplaced.

3. ANOTHER might be calculated for each
feafon of the year; illuftrating the wifdom, the
power, and the benevolence of Providence.—How
idle to forego fuch fair and peaceable fubjects,
for

for the fake of widening the breach betwixt grace and works, predeftination and election, folving the revelations, or afcertaining the precife nature of Urim and Thummim ?

It is a common argument amongft divines, in the behalf of a religious life, that a contrary behaviour has fuch, confequences when we come to die. It is indeed true, but feems an argument of a fubordinate kind : the article of death is more frequently of fhort duration. Is it not a ftronger perfuafive, that virtue makes us happy daily, and removes the fear of death from our lives antecedently, than that it fmooths the pillow of a death-bed ?

It is a queftion, whether the remaining fuperftitions among the vulgar of the Englifh nation ought wholly to be removed ? The notion of a ghoft's appearance for the difcovery of murder, or any flagrant act of injuftice ; "That what " is got over the devil's back, will be fpent un- " der his belly ;" "That cards are the devil's " books," &c.

If there be numbers of people that murder and devour their fpecies ; that have contradictory notions of beauty ; that have deemed it meritorious to offer up human facrifices, to leave their parents in deferts of wild beafts, to expofe their offspring as foon as born, &c. &c. there fhould feem to be no univerfal moral fenfe, and, of confequence, none.

It is not now, " We have feen his ftar in the " eaft," but, " We have feen the ftar on his " breaft, and are come to worfhip him."

It is faid, and I believe juftly enough, that crimes appear lefs hainous to a perfon that is about committing them, than to his confcience afterwards. Is then the crime to be imputed to him in the degree he forefaw it, or in that he re-flects upon it ? Perhaps the one and the other may incline towards an extreme.

The word *religio* amongft the Romans, and the word *church* among the Chriftians, feem to have more interpretations than almoft any other. *Malus procidit, ea religione moti.* — Livy, p. 1150. vol. 2. here *religion* feems to mean *prodigy.* — *Si quis tale facrum folenne duceret, nec fe fine religione et piaculo id omittere poffe.* Livy, 1157. here it feemingly means *impiety*.; *piaculum* being fuch an offence as required expiatory facrifices.

> *Tantum religio potuit fuadere malorum !*

here it means *fuperftition*, as it does often in Lucretius.

The pope's wanton excommunications, his capricious pardon of fins, his enormous indulgences, and other particulars of like nature, fhew that (whatever religions may practife cruelty) it is peculiarly the church that makes a jeft of God Almighty.

The word *church* has thefe different fenfes.

1. A set of people ordained to affift at divine fervice.

2. The members of a certain religious profeffion, including clergy and laity.

3. A large piece of building dedicated to the
fervice

fervice of God, and furnifhed with proper conveniencies for thofe who meet to worfhip him.

4. A body of people who too frequently ha-
rafs and infeft the laity according to law, and
who conceal their real names under that of a
fpiritual court.

How ready have all nations been, after having allowed a proper portion of laud and praife
to their own abilities, to attribute their fuccefs in
war to the peculiar favour of a juft Providence !
Perhaps this conftruction, as it is often applied,
argues more of prefumption than gratitude.   In
the firft place, fuch is the partiality of the human heart, that, perhaps, two hoftile nations may
alike rely upon the juftice of their caufe ; and
which of the two has the better claim to it, none
but Providence can itfelf difcover.   In the next,
it fhould be obferved, that fuccefs by no means
demonftrates juftice.   Again, we muft not wholly forget to confider, that fuccefs may be no
more than a means of deftruction,   And laftly, fuppofing fuccefs to be really and abfolutely
good, do we find that individuals are always favoured with it in proportion to their defert ; and
if not individuals, why muft we then fuppofe it
to be the uniform recompenfe of fociety?

It is often given as a reafon why it is incumbent on God Almighty's juftice, to punifh or reward focieties in this world, becaufe hereafter
they cannot be punifhed or rewarded on account
of their diffolution.   It is indeed true, that human vengeance muft act frequently in the grofs ;
and whenever a government declares war againft

a foreign fociety, or finds it needful to chaftife any part of its own, muft of neceffity involve fome innocent individuals with the guilty. But it does not appear fo evident, that an omnifcient and omnipotent Being, who knows the fecrets of all hearts, and is able to make a diftinction in his punifhments, will judge his unhappy creatures by thefe indifcriminate and imperfect laws.

Societies then are to be confidered as the cafual or arbitrary affortments of human inftitution. To fuppofe that God Almighty will, by means of punifhments, often called judgments, deftroy them promifcuoufly, is to fuppofe that he will regulate his government according to the cabals of human wifdom. I mean to be underftood here, with regard to what are called judgments, or, in other words, preternatural interpofitions of Providence. In a natural way, the conftitution of the univerfe requires, that the good muft often fuffer with the bad part of fociety. But in regard to judgments upon whole bodies, (which we have days appointed to deprecate), let us introduce a cafe which may ferve to illuftrate the improbability.

Societies, I fuppofe then, are not divine, but human bundles.

Imagine a man to mix a large quantity of fand and gunpowder, then parcel out the compofition into different heaps, and apply fire to them feparately. The fire, it is very obvious, would take no notice of the bundles; would by no means confume, here and there, a bundle in

the

the grofs, but would affect that part of every portion that was combuftible.

It may fpecioufly enough be faid, what greater injuftice is it to punifh a fociety promifcuoufly, than to involve an innocent fon in the punifhment due to a finful father? To this I anfwer, the natural fyftem (which we need not doubt, upon the whole, is right) occafions both the good and bad to fuffer many times indifcriminately. But they go much further.—They fay; God, as it were, interferes in oppofition to the fettled courfe of things, to punifh and include focieties in one promifcuous vengeance. Were he to inflict extraordinary punifhments diftinct from thofe which fin entails upon us, he furely would not regulate them by mere human affortments, but would make the jufter diftinction of good and evil individuals.

Neither do I fee why it is fo neceffary that focieties, either here or hereafter, fhould be punifhed as focieties. *The foul that finneth, it fhall die.*

How happy may a lord bifhop render a peafant at the hour of death, by beftowing on him his bleffing, and giving him affurance of falvation? It is the fame with regard to religious opinions in general. They may be confirmed and eftablifhed to their hearts content, becaufe they affent implicitly to the opinions of men who they think fhould know. A perfon of diftinguifhed parts and learning has no fuch advantages: friendlefs, wavering, folitary, and, through his very fituation, incapable of much affiftance.

If

If the ruftic's tenor of behaviour approach nearer to the brutes, he alfo appears to approach nearer to their happinefs.

You pray for happinefs.—Confider the fituation or difpofition of your mind at the time, and you will find it naturally tends to produce it.

In travelling one contrives to allow day-light for the worfe part of the road. But in life, how, hard is it that every unhappinefs feems united towards the clofe of our journey! Pain, fatigue, and want of fpirits, when fpirits are more immediately neceffary to our fupport, of which nothing can fupply the place befide religion and philofophy. But then the foundation muft be laid in meditation and inquiry; at an unmolefted feafon, when our faculties are ftrong and vigorous; or the tempeft will moft probably throw down the fuperftructure.

How is a man faid to be guilty of incredulity? Are there not fizes of underftandings adapted to the different forts, and as it were fizes of narrations?

Conscience is adfcititious; I mean influenced by conviction, which may be well or ill grounded; therefore no certain teft of truth, but at moft times a very faithful and a very prudent admonitor.

The attraction of bodies, and focial affection of minds, feem in many refpects analogous.

Attractions of either kind are lefs perfpicuous, and lefs perceptible, through a variety of counter-attractions that diminifh their effect. Were two perfons to meet in Ifpahan, though quite ftrangers to each other here, would they

not

not go near to feel a kind of friendſhip, on the
ſingle ſcore of their being Engliſhmen ? Would
they not paſs a cheerful evening together over
rice and ſherbet ?—In like manner, ſuppoſe two
or three contemporaries only to meet on the ſur-
face of the globe amid myriads of perſons of all
other ages whatſoever, would they not diſcover a
mutual tenderneſs, even though they had been
enemies when living ? What then remains, but
that we revive the memory of ſuch relations now,
in order to quicken our benevolence ? That we
are all countrymen, is a conſideration that is more
commonly inculcated, and limits our benevolence
to a ſmaller number alſo. That we are contemporaries, and perſons whom future hiſtory ſhall
unite, who, great part of us, however imperceptibly, receive and confer reciprocal benefits ; this,
with every other circumſtance that tends to
heighten our philanthropy, ſhould be brought
to mind as much as poſſible, during our abode
upon earth. Hereafter, it may be juſt and re-
quiſite to comprehend all ages of mankind.

THE beſt notion we can conceive of God, may
be, that he is to the creation what the ſoul is to
the body :

—*Deus eſt quodcunque vides, ubicunque moveris.*

WHAT is man, while we reflect upon a Deity,
whoſe very words are works, and all whoſe
works are wonders !

PRAYER is not uſed to inform, for God is om-
niſcient ; not to move compaſſion, for God is
without paſſions ; not to ſhew our gratitude, for
God knows our hearts. May not a man that
                                    has

has true notions, be a pious man though he be filent ?

To honour God is to conceive right notions of him, fays fome ancient that I have forgot.

I know not how Mr. Pope's affertion is con-fiftent with the fcheme of a particular provi-dence :

———————*The almighty caufe*
Acts not by partial, but by general laws.

What one underftands by a general provi-dence is that attention of the Almighty to the works of his creation, by which they purfue their original courfe, without deviating into fuch ec-centric motions as muft immediately tend to the deftruction of it. Thus a philofopher is enabled to foretell eclipfes with precifion.; and a ftone thrown upward, drops uniformly to the ground. Thus an injury awakes refentment, and a good office endears to us our benefactor. And it feems no unworthy idea of Omnipotence, perhaps, to fuppofe he at firft conftituted a fyftem that ftood in no need either of his counteracting or fuf-pending the firft laws of motion.

But after all the mind remains, and we can fhew it to be either impoffible or improbable that God directs the will. Now, whether the di-vine Being occafions a ruin to fall miraculoufly, or in direct oppofition to the ordinary laws of nature, upon the head of Chartres, —or whether he inclines Chartres to go near a wall whofe centre of gravity is unfupported, makes no ma-terial difference.

On

ON TASTE.

I BELIEVE that, generally fpeaking, perfons eminent in one branch of tafte have the principles of the reft; and to try this, I have often folicited a ftranger to hum a tune, and have feldom failed of fuccefs. This, however, does not extend to talents beyond the fphere of tafte; and Handel was evidently wrong, when he fancied himfelf born to command a troop of horfe.

MANKIND, in general, may be divided into perfons of underftanding, and perfons of genius; each of which will admit of many fubordinate degrees. By perfons of underftanding, I mean perfons of found judgment, formed for mathematical deductions, and clear argumentation. By perfons of genius, I would characterife thofe in whom true and genuine fancy predominates, and this whether affifted or not by cultivation.

I HAVE thought that genius and judgment may, in fome refpects, be reprefented by a liquid and a folid. The former is, generally fpeaking, remarkable for its fenfibility, but then lofes its impreffion foon; the latter is lefs fufceptible of impreffion, but retains it longer.

DIVIDING the world into an hundred parts, I am apt to believe the calculation might be thus adjufted.

Pedants	15
Perfons of common fenfe	40
	Wits

Wits ———— ———— ———— 15
Fools ———— . ———— 15
Perfons of a wild uncultivated tafte — 10
Perfons of original tafte, improved by art 5

THERE is hardly any thing fo uncommon as a true native tafte improved by education.

THE object of tafte is corporeal beauty : for though there is manifeftly a το πρεπον, a *pulchrum*, an *honeftum*, and *decorum*, in moral actions ; and although a man of tafte that is not virtuous, commits a greater violence upon his fentiments than any other perfon ; yet, in the ordinary courfe of fpeaking, a perfon is not termed a man of tafte, merely becaufe he is a man of virtue.

ALL beauty may be divided into abfolute and relative, and what is compounded of both.

IT is not uncommon to hear a modern Quixote infift upon the fuperiority of his idol or Dulcinea ; and, not content to pay his own tribute of adoration, demand that of others in favour of her accomplifhments. Thofe of grave and fober fenfe cannot avoid wondering at a difference of opinions, which are in truth fupported by no criterion.

EVERY one, therefore, ought to fix fome meafure of beauty, before he grows eloquent upon the fubject.

EVERY thing feems to derive its pretenfions to beauty, on account of its colour, fmoothnefs, variety, uniformity, partial refemblance to fomething elfe, proportion, or fuitablenefs to the end

proposed,

propofed, fome connection of ideas, or a mixture of all thefe.

As to the beauty of colours, their prefent effect feems in proportion to their impulfe; and fcarlet, were it not for habit, would affect an Indian before all other colours.

RESEMBLANCES wrought by art, pictures, buftoes, ftatues, pleafe.

COLUMNS, proportioned to their incumbent weight; but herein we fuppofe homogeneous materials; it is otherwife, in cafe we know that a column is made of iron.

HABIT herein feems to have an influence to which we can affix no bounds. Suppofe the generality of mankind formed with a mouth from ear to ear, and that it were requifite in point of refpiration, would not the prefent make of mouths have fubjected a man to the name of Bocha chica?

IT is probable, that a clown would require more colour in his Chloe's face, than a courtier.

WE may fee daily the ftrange effects of habit in refpect of fafhion. To what colours or proportions does it not reconcile us!

CONCEIT is falfe tafte, and very widely different from no tafte at all.

BEAUTY of perfon fhould, perhaps, be eftimated according to the proportion it bears to fuch a make and features as are moft likely to produce the love of the oppofite fex. The look of dignity, the look of wifdom, the look of delicacy and refinement, feem, in fome meafure, foreign. Perhaps the appearance of fenfibility

may

may be one ingredient, and that of health another. At leaft, a cadaverous countenance is the moft difgufting in the world.

I know not if one reafon of the different opinions concerning beauty be not owing to felf-love. People are apt to form fome criterion from their own perfons or poffeffions. A tall perfon approves the look of a folio or octavo ; a fquare thick-fet man is more delighted with a quarto. This inftance, at leaft, may ferve to explain what I intend.

I believe it fometimes happens that a perfon may have what the artifts call an ear and an eye, without tafte : For inftance, a man may fometimes have a quicknefs in diftinguifhing the fimilitude or difference of lines and founds, without any fkill to give the proper preference betwixt the combinations of them.

Taste produces different effects upon different complexions. It confifts, as I have often obferved, in the appetite and the difcernment ; then moft properly fo called, when they are united in equal proportions.

Where the difcernment is predominant, a perfon is pleafed with fewer objects, and requires perfection in what he fees. Where the appetite prevails, he is fo much attached to beauty, that he feels a gratification in every degree in which it is manifefted. I frankly own myfelf to be of this latter clafs : I love painting and ftatuary fo well, as to be not undelighted with moderate performances.

The reafon people vary in their opinions of

a

a portrait, I mean, with regard to the resemblance it bears to the original, seems no other than that they lay stress on different features in the original ; and this different stress is owing to different complexions of mind.

PEOPLE of little or no taste commend a person for its corpulency. I cannot see why an excrescence of belly, cheek, or chin, should be deemed more beautiful than a wen on any other part of the body. Through a connection of ideas, it may form the beauty of a pig or an ox.

THERE seems a pretty exact analogy between the objects and the senses. Some tunes, some tastes, some visible objects, please at first, and that only ; others only by degrees, and then long.—(Raspberry-jelly—Green-tea—Alley-Croaker—Air in Ariadne—A baron's robe—and a bishop's lawn). Perhaps some of these instances may be ill enough chosen, but the thing is true.

TUNES with words please me the more in proportion as they approach nearer to the natural accent of the words to which they are assigned. Scotch tunes often end high : their language does the same.

To how very great a degree the appearance of health alone is beauty, I am not able to determine. I presume the most regular and well-proportioned form of limbs and features is at the same time the most healthful one ; the fittest to perform the functions and operations of the body. If so, a perfectly healthful form is a

VOL. II.   U   perfectly

perfectly beautiful form.—Health is beauty, and the moft perfect health is the moft perfect beauty. To have recourfe to experience ; the moft fickly and cadaverous countenance is the leaft provocative to love, or rather the moft inconfiftent with it. A florid look, to appear beautiful, muft be the bloom of health, and not the glow of a fever.

An obvious connection may be traced betwixt moral and phyfical beauty, the love of fymmetry and the love of virtue, an elegant tafte and perfect honefty. We may, we muft, rife from the love of natural to that of moral beauty. Such is the conclufion of Plato, and of my Lord Shaftefbury.

Where-ever there is a want of tafte, we generally obferve a love of money, and cunning ; and whenever tafte prevails, a want of prudence, and an utter difregard to money.

Taste (or a juft relifh of beauty) feems to diftinguifh us from the brute creation, as much as intellect, or reafon. We do not find that brutes have any fenfation of this fort. A bull is goaded by the love of fex in general, without the leaft appearance of any diftinction in favour of the more beautiful individual. Accordingly men devoid of tafte are in a great meafure indifferent as to make, complexion, feature ; and find a difference of fex fufficient to excite their paffion in all its fervour. It is not thus where there is a tafte for beauty, either accurate or erroneous. The perfon of a good tafte requires real beauty in the object of his paffion ; and the

perfon

perſon of bad taſte requires ſomething which he ſubſtitutes in the place of beauty.

PERSONS of taſte, it has been aſſerted, are alſo the beſt qualified to diſtinguiſh, and the moſt prone to admire moral virtue : nor does it invalidate this maxim, that their practice does not correſpond. The power of acting virtuouſly depends in a great meaſure upon withſtanding a preſent, and perhaps ſenſual gratification, for the ſake of a more diſtant, and intellectual ſatisfaction. Now, as perſons of fine taſte are men of the ſtrongeſt ſenſual appetites, it happens that, in balancing preſent and future, they are apt enough to allow an unreaſonable advantage to the former. On the other hand, a more phlegmatic character may, with no greater ſelf-denial, allow the future fairer play. But let us wave the merely ſenſual indulgences ; and let us conſider the man of taſte in regard to points of *meum* and *tuum* ; in regard to the virtues of forgiveneſs ; in regard to charity, compaſſion, munificence, and magnanimity ; and we cannot fail to vote his taſte the glorious triumph which it deſerves.

THERE is a kind of counter-taſte, founded on ſurpriſe and curioſity, which maintains a ſort of rivalſhip with the true ; and may be expreſſed by the name *Concetto*. Such is the fondneſs of ſome perſons for a knife-haft made from the royal oak, or a tobacco-ſtopper from a mulberry-tree of Shakeſpear's own planting. It gratifies an empty curioſity. Such is the caſual reſemblance of Apollo and the nine Muſes in a piece

of

of agate ; a dog expreffed in feathers, or a wood-
cock in mohair.   They ferve to give furprife.
But a juft fancy will no more efteem a picture,
becaufe it proves to be produced by fhells, than
a writer would prefer a pen, becaufe a perfon
made it with his toes.   In all fuch cafes, difficulty
fhould not be allowed to give a cafting weight ;
nor a needle be confidered as a painter's inftrument, when he is fo much better furnifhed with
a pencil *.

PERHAPS no print, or even painting, is capable of producing a figure anfwerable to the idea
which poetry or hiftory has given us of great
men : A Cicero, for inftance, an Homer, a Cato,
or an Alexander.   The fame, perhaps, is true of
the grandeur of fome ancient buildings.—And
the reafon is, that the effects of a pencil are diftinct and limited, whereas the defcriptions of
the pen leave the imagination room to expatiate ;
and Burke has made it extremely obvious, that
indiftinctnefs of outline is one fource of the
fublime.

WHAT an abfurdity is it, in the framing even
prints, to fuffer a margin of white paper to appear beyond the ground, deftroying half the
relievo the lights are intended to produce ?
Frames ought to contraft with paintings, or to
appear as diftinct as poffible : for which reafon,

---

* Cornelius Ketel born at Gonda in 1548; landed in England
1573; fettled at Amfterdam 1581; took it into his head to
grow famous by painting with his fingers inftead of pencils.—
The whim took—his fuccefs increafed—his fingers appearing
too eafy tools, he then undertook to paint with his feet.——
See H. Walpole's book of painters.

frames.

frames of wood inlaid, or otherwife variegated with colours, are lefs fuitable than gilt ones, which exhibiting an appearance of metal afford the beft contraft with colour.

The peculiar expreffion in fome portraits is owing to the greater or lefs manifeftation of the foul in fome of the features.

There is, perhaps, a fublime and a beautiful in the very make of a face, exclufive of any particular expreffion of the foul ; or, at leaft, not expreffive of any other than a tame difpaffionate one. We fee often what the world calls regular features, and a good complexion, almoft totally unanimated by any difcovery of the temper or underftanding. Whenever the regularity of feature, beauty of complexion, the ftrong expreffion of fagacity and generofity, concur in one face, the features are irrefiftible.

But even here it is to be obferved, that a fort of fympathy has a prodigious bias.—Thus a penfive beauty, with regular features and complexion, will have the preference with a fpectator of the penfive caft ; and fo of the reft.

The foul appears to me to difcover herfelf moft in the mouth and eyes ; with this difference, that the mouth feems the more expreffive of the temper, and the eye of the underftanding.

Is a portrait, fuppofing it as like as can be to the perfon for whom it is drawn, a more or lefs beautiful object than the original face ? I fhould think, a perfect face muft be much more pleafing than any reprefentation of it ; and a fet of ugly features much more ugly than the moft ex-

act.

act refemblance that can be drawn of them. Painting can do much by means of fhades, but not equal the force of real relievo; on which account it may be the advantage of bad features to have their effect diminifhed; but furely, never can be the intereft of good ones.

Softness of manner feems to be in painting, what fmoothnefs of fyllables is in language; affecting the fenfe of fight or hearing, previous to any correfpondent paffion.

The " theory of agreeable fenfations" founds them upon the greateft activity or exercife an object occafions to the fenfes, without proceeding to fatigue. Violent contrafts are upon the footing of roughnefs or inequality.—Harmony or fimilitude, on the other hand, are fomewhat cogenial to fmoothnefs.—In other words, thefe two recommend themfelves, the one to our love of action, the other to our love of reft. A medium, therefore, may be moft agreeable to the generality.

An harmony in colours feems as requifite as a variety of lines feems neceffary, to the pleafure we expect from outward forms. The lines, indeed, fhould be well varied; but yet the oppofite fides of any thing fhould fhew a balance, or an appearance of equal quantity, if we would ftrive to pleafe a well-conftituted tafte.

It is evident enough to me, that perfons often occur who may be faid to have an ear to mufic, and an eye for proportions in vifible objects, who, neverthelefs, can hardly be faid to have a relifh or tafte for either. I mean that a perfon

may

may distinguish notes and tones to a nicety, and yet not give a discerning choice to what is preferable in music. The same in objects of sight.

On the other hand, they cannot have a proper feeling of beauty or harmony, without a power of discriminating those notes and proportions on which harmony and beauty so fully depend.

What is said, in a treatise lately published, for beauty's being more common than deformity (and seemingly with excellent reason), may be also said for virtue's being more common than vice.

Quere, Whether beauty do not as much require an opposition of lines, as it does an harmony of colours.?

The passion for antiquity, as such, seems in some measure opposite to the taste for beauty or perfection. It is rather the foible of a lazy and pusillanimous disposition, looking back and resting with pleasure on the steps by which we have arrived thus far, than the bold and enterprising spirit of a genius, whose ambition fires him only to reach the goal ; such as is described (on another occasion) in the zealous and active charioteer of Horace.

—— hunc atque hunc superare laboret,
Instat equis auriga suos vincentibus ; illum
Praeteritum temnens, extremos inter euntem.

Again, the

Nil actum reputans, si quid restaret agendum,

is

is the leaft applicable of any character to a
mere antiquarian ; who, inftead of endeavouring to improve or to excel, contents himfelf, perhaps, with difcovering the very name of a firft
inventor, or with tracing back an art that
is flourifhing, to the very firft fource of its original deformity.

I have heard it claimed by adepts in mufic,
that the pleafure it imparts to a natural ear,
which owes little or nothing to cultivation, is
by no means to be compared to what they feel
themfelves from the moft perfect compofition.—
The ftate of the queftion may be beft explained
by a recourfe to objects that are analogous.—Is a
country-fellow lefs ftruck with beauty than a
philofopher or an anatomift who knows how that
beauty is produced ? Surely no. On the other
hand, an attention to the caufe may fomewhat
interfere with the attention to the effect.—They
may indeed feel a pleafure of another fort.—The
faculty of reafon may obtain fome kind of balance, for what the more fenfible faculty of the
imagination lofes.

I am much inclined to fuppofe our ideas of
beauty depend greatly upon habit.—What I mean
is, upon the familiarity with objects which we
happen to have feen fince we came into the
world.—Our tafte for uniformity, from what we
have obferved in the individual parts of nature,
a man, a tree, a beaft, a bird, or infect, &c. our
tafte for regularity from what is within our power
to obferve in the feveral perfections of the whole
fyftem.

A

A LANDSCAPE, for inftance, is always irregular ; and to ufe regularity in painting or gardening, would make our work unnatural and difagreeable.   Thus we allow beauty to the different, and almoft oppofite proportions of all animals.

THERE is, I think, a beauty in fome forms, independent of any ufe to which they can be applied.   I know not whether this may not be refolved into fmoothnefs of furface, with variety to a certain degree, that is comprehenfible without much difficulty.

As to the dignity of colours, Quere, Whether thofe that affect the eye moft forcibly, for inftance, fcarlet, may not claim the firft place ; allowing their beauty to cloy fooneft ; and other colours, the next, according to their impulfe ; allowing them to produce a more durable pleafure ?

IT may be convenient to divide beauty into the abfolute, and the relative   Abfolute is that above mentioned.   Relative is that by which an object, or part of an object, pleafes, through the relation it bears to fome other.

OUR tafte of beauty is, perhaps, compounded of all the ideas that have entered the imagination from our birth.   This feems to occafion the different opinion that prevails concerning it. For inftance, a foreign eye efteems thofe features and dreffes handfome which we think deformed.

Is it not then likely that thofe who have feen moft objects throughout the univerfe, *cateris paribus,*

paribus, will be the most impartial judges ? because they will judge truest of the general proportion which was intended by the Creator, and
is best.

THE beauty of most objects is partly of the
absolute, and partly of the relative kind. A
Corinthian pillar has some beauty dependent on
its variety and smoothness, which I would call
absolute ; it has also a relative beauty, dependent
on its tapernefs and foliage ; which authors say
was first copied from the leaves of plants, and
the shape of a tree,

UNIFORMITY should, perhaps, be added as
another source of absolute beauty, (when it appears in one single object). I do not know any o-
ther reason, but that it renders the whole more
easily comprehended. It seems that nature herself considers it as beauty, as the external parts of
the human frame are made uniform to please the
sight ; which is rarely the case of the internal,
that are not seen.

HUTCHESON determines absolute beauty to
depend on this, and on variety ; and says it is
in a compound ratio of both. Thus an octagon
excels a square ; and a square, a figure of unequal sides. But carry variety to an extreme, and
it loses its effect. For instance, multiply the number of angles till the mind loses the uniformity
of parts, and the figure is less pleasing : or, as
it approaches nearer to a round, it may be said
to be robbed of its variety.

BUT, amidst all these eulogiums of variety, it is
proper to observe that novelty sometimes requires

a.

a little abatement. I mean, that some degree of familiarity introduces a discovery of relative beauty, more than adequate to the bloom of novelty. —This is now and then obvious in the features of a face, the air of some tunes, and the flavour of some dishes. In short, it requires some familiarity to become acquainted · with the relation that parts bear unto the whole, or one object to another.

VARIETY in the same object, where the beauty does not depend on imitation, (which is the case in foliage, bustoes, basso-relievos, painting), requires uniformity. For instance, an octagon is much more beautiful than a figure of unequal sides, which is at once various and disagreeable.

VERSES

V E R S E S

T O

Mr S H E N S T O N E.

✦✦✦✦✦✦✦✦✦✦✦✦✦✦✦✦✦✦✦✦✦✦✦✦✦✦✦✦✦✦✦✦✦✦✦✦✦✦✦

Written at a ferme ornée, near Birmingham,

By the late Lady LUXBOROUGH.

'TIS Nature here bids pleafing fcenes arife,
    And wifely gives them Cynthio to revife ;
To veil each blemifh, brighten every grace,
Yet ftill preferve the lovely parent's face.
How well the bard obeys, each valley tells ;
Thefe lucid ftreams, gay meads, and lonely cells ;
Where modeft art in filence lurks conceal'd,
While nature fhines fo gracefully reveal'd,
That fhe triumphant claims the total plan,
And, with frefh pride, adopts the work of man.

To

To WILLIAM SHENSTONE, *Esq; at the* LEASOWES.

By *Mr* GRAVES *of* CLAVERTON.

Vellem in amicitia fic erraremus ! HOR.

SEE ! the tall youth, by partial fate's decree,
To affluence born, and from reftraint fet free.
Eager he feeks the fcenes of gay refort,
The mall, the rout, the play-houfe, and the court :
Soon for fome varnifh'd nymph of dubious fame,
Or powder'd peerefs, counterfeits a flame.
Behold him now, enraptur'd, fwear and figh,
Drefs, dance, drink, revel, all he knows not why ;
Till, by kind fate reftor'd to country-air,
He marks the rofes of fome rural fair :
Smit with her unaffected, native charms,
A real paffion foon his bofom warms ;
And wak'd from idle dreams, he takes a wife,
And taftes the genuine happinefs of life.

Thus in the vacant feafon of the year,
Some Templar gay begins his wild career.
From feat to feat o'er pompous fcenes he flies,
Views all with equal wonder and furprife ;
Till fick of domes, arcades, and temples grown,
He hies fatigu'd, not fatisfy'd, to town.
Yet if fome kinder genius point his way
To where the mufes o'er thy Leafowes ftray,
Charm'd with the fylvan beauties of the place,
Where art affumes the fweets of nature's face,

VOL. II.   X   Each

Each hill, each dale, each confecrated grove,
Each lake, and falling ftream his rapture move.
Like the fage captive in Calypfo's grott,
The cares, the pleafures of the world forgot,
Of calm content he hails the genuine fphere,
And longs to dwell a blifsful hermit here.

*VERSES received by the poft, from a
Lady unknown,* 1761.

HEalth to the bard in Leafowes' happy groves ; -
    Health, and fweet converfe with the mufe
        he loves !
The humbleft vot'ry of the tuneful nine,
With trembling hand attempts her artlefs line,
In numbers fuch as untaught nature brings ;
As flow, fpontaneous, like thy native fprings.

    But ah ! what airy forms around me rife !
The ruffet mountain glows with richer dies ;
In circling dance a pigmy croud appear,
And hark ! an infant voice falutes my ear.
" Mortal, thy aim we know, thy tafk approve ;
" His merit, honour, and his genius love :
" For us what verdant carpets has he fpread,
" Where nightly we our myftic mazes tread ?
" For us, each fhady grove, and rural feat,
" His falling ftreams, and flowing numbers fweet :
" Didft thou not mark, amid the winding dell,
" What tuneful verfe adorns the moffy cell ?
" There every fairy of our fprightly train
" Reforts, to blefs the woodland and the plain.
" There, as we move, unbidden beauties glow,
" The green turf brightens, and the violets blow ;
" And there, with thought fublime we blefs the
        fwain,
" Nor we infpire, nor he attends, in vain."

Go, fimple rhymer ! bear this meffage true ;
The truths that Fairies dictate none fhall rue.
Say to the bard in Leafowes' happy grove,
Whom Dryads honour, and whom Fairies love—
" Content thyfelf no longer that thy lays,
" By others fofter'd, lend to others praife ;
" No longer to the fav'ring world refufe
" The welcome treafures of thy polifh'd mufe ;
" The fcatter'd blooms that boaft thy valu'd name,
" Collect, unite, and give the wreath to fame ;
" Ne'er can thy virtues, or thy verfe engage
" More folid praife than in this happieft age,
" When fenfe and merit's cherifh'd by the throne,
" And each illuftrious privilege their own.
" Tho' modeft be thy gentle mufe, I ween,
" O lead her blufhing from the daify'd green,   }
" A fit attendant on Britannia's Queen.

Ye fportive elves, as faithful I relate
Th' intrufted mandates of your fairy-ftate,
Vifit thefe wilds again with nightly care ;
So fhall my kine, of all the herd, repair
In healthful plight to fill the copious pail ;
My fheep lie pent with fafety in the dale :
My poultry fear no robber in the rooft ;
My linen more than common whitenefs boaft :
Let order, peace, and houfewifery be mine ;
SHENSTONE, be fancy, fame, and fortune thine.

COTSWOULDIA.

On the difcovery of an echo at EDGBASTON.

By —— ——.

HA ! what art thou, whofe voice unknown
 Pours on thefe plains its tender moan ?
Art thou the nymph in SHENSTONE's dale,
Who doft with plaintive note bewail
That he forfakes th' Aonian maids,
To court inconftant rills and fhades ?
Mourn not, fweet nymphs, alas, in vain
Do they invite, and thou complain——

 Yet while he woo'd the gentle throng,
With liquid lay, and melting fong,
The lift'ning herd around him ftray'd,
In wanton frifk the lambkins play'd,
And every Naïad ceas'd to lave
Her azure limbs amid the wave.
The graces danc'd ; the rofy band
Of fmiles and loves went hand in hand ;
And purple pleafures ftrew'd the way
With fweeteft flowers ; and every ray
Of each fond Mufe with rapture fir'd,
To glowing thoughts his breaft infpir'd.
The hills rejoic'd, the valleys rung,
All nature fmil'd while SHENSTONE fung.

 So charm'd his lay ; but now no more —
Ah ! why doft thou repeat— " no more ?"
X 3

Ev'n

Ev'n now he hies to deck the grove,
To deck the fcene the Mufes love ;
And foon again will own their fway,
And thou refound the peerlefs lay,
And with immortal numbers fill
Each rocky cave, and vocal hill.

V E R S E S

VERSES by Mr Dodsley, *on his firſt*
arrival at the Leasowes, 1754.

" HOW ſhall I fix my wand'ring eye ? Where
"   find
" The ſource of this inchantment ? Dwells it in
" The woods ? Or waves there not a magic wand
" O'er the tranſlucent waters ? Sure, unſeen,
" Some fav'ring power directs the happy lines
" That ſketch theſe beauties ; ſwells the riſing hills
" And ſcoops the dales to nature's fineſt forms,
" Vague, undetermin'd, infinite ; untaught
" By line or compaſs, yet ſupremely fair."

So ſpake Philenor, as with raptur'd gaze
He travers'd Damon's farm. From diſtant plains
He ſought his friend's abode : nor had the fame
Of that new-form'd Arcadia reach'd his ear.

And thus the ſwain, as o'er each hill and dale,
Thro' lawn or thicket he purſu'd his way.
" What is it gilds the verdure of theſe meads
" With hues more bright than fancy paints the
        flow'rs
" Of Paradiſe ? What Naïad's guiding hand
" Leads, thro' the broider'd vale, theſe lucid rills,
" That, murmuring as they flow, bear melody
" Along their banks ; and, thro' the vocal ſhades,
" Improve the muſic of the woodland choir ?
" What penſive Dryad rais'd yon ſolemn grove,
" Where minds contemplative, at cloſe of day
                    " Retiring,

" Retiring, mufe o'er nature's various works,
" Her wonders venerate, or her fweets enjoy—
" What room for doubt ? Some rural deity
" Prefiding, fcatters o'er th' unequal lawns,
" In beauteous wildnefs, yon fair fpreading trees ;
" And, mingling woods and waters, hills and
    dales,
" And herds and bleating flocks, domeftic fowl,
" And thofe that fwim the lake, fees rifing round'
" More pleafing landfcapes than in 'Tempe's vale
" Peneus water'd.   Yes, fome fylvan god
" Spreads wide the varied profpect ; waves the
    woods,
" Lifts the proud hills, and clears the fhining lakes ;
" While from the congregated waters pour'd,
" The burfting torrent tumbles down the fteep
" In foaming fury ; fierce, irregular,
" Wild, interrupted, crofs'd with rocks and roots,
" And interwoven trees ; till foon abforb'd,
" An op'ning cavern all its rage entombs.
" So vanifh human glories ! Such the pomp
" Of fwelling warriours, of ambitious kings,
" Who fret and ftrut their hour upon the ftage
" Of bufy life, and then are heard no more.

 " Yes, 'tis enchantment all—And fee, the fpells,
" The powerful incantations, magic verfe,
" Infcrib'd on every tree, alcove, or urn,—
" Spells !—Incantations !—ah, my tuneful friend ?
" Thine are the numbers ! thine the wondrous
    work !—
" Yes, great magician ! now I read thee right,
" And lightly weigh all forcery but thine.
       " No

" No Naïad's leading ftep conducts the rill ;
" Nor fylvan god prefiding fkirts the lawn
" In beauteous wildnefs, with fair fpreading trees ;
" Nor magic wand has circumfcrib'd the fcene.
" 'Tis thine own tafte, thy genius that prefides,
" Nor needs there other deity, nor needs
" More potent fpells than they."   No more the
    fwain,
For lo, his Damon, o'er the tufted lawn
Advancing, leads him to the focial dome.

VERSES *written at the gardens of* WIL-
LIAM SHENSTONE, *Efq; near Birmingham,*
1756.

Ille terrarum mihi praeter omnes
Angulus ridet. HOR.

WOULD you thefe lov'd receffes trace,
 And view fair nature's modeft face ?
See her in every field-flower bloom ?
O'er every thicket fhed perfume ?
By verdant groves, and vocal hills,
By moffy grotts, near purling rills,
Where-e'er you turn your wond'ring eyes,
Behold her win without difguife.

 What tho' no pageant trifles here,
As in the glare of courts, appear ;
Tho' rarely here be heard the name
Of rank or title, power or fame ;
Yet, if ingenuous be your mind,
A blifs more pure and unconfin'd
Your ftep attends.—Draw freely nigh,
And meet the bard's benignant eye :
On him no pedant forms await,
No proud referve fhuts up his gate ;
No fpleen, no party-views controul
That warm benevolence of foul,
Which prompts the friendly gen'rous part,
Regardlefs of each venal art ;
Regardlefs of the world's acclaim,
And courteous with no felfifh aim.

         Draw

Draw freely nigh, and welcome find,
If not the coftly, yet the kind.
O he will lead you to the cells
Where every mufe and virtue dwells,
Where the green Dryads guard his woods,
Where the blue Naïads guide his floods ;
Where all the fifter-graces gay,
That fhap'd his walk's meand'ring way,
Stark-naked, or but wreath'd with flowers,
Lie flumb'ring foft beneath his bowers.

Wak'd by the ftock-dove's melting ftrain,
Behold them rife ! and, with the train'
Of nymphs that haunt the ftream or grove;
Or o'er the flowery champian rove,
Join hand in hand—attentive gaze—
And mark the dance's myftic maze.

" Such is the WAVING LINE," they· cry,
" For ever dear to fancy's eye !
" Yon ftream that wanders down the dale,
" The fpiral wood, the winding vale,
" The path which wrought with hidden fkill,
" Slow twining fcales yon diftant hill
" With fir invefted—all combine
" To recommend the WAVING LINE.

" The wreathed rod of Bacchus fair,
" The ringlets of Apollo's hair,
" The wand by Maia's offspring borne,
" The fmooth volutes of Ammon's horn,
" The ftrufture of the Cyprian dame,
" And each fair female's beauteous frame,
                    " Shew,

" Shew, to the pupils of defign,
" The triumphs of the WAVING LINE."

  Then gaze, and mark that union fweet,
Where fair convex and concave meet ;
And while, quick fhifting as you ftray,
The vivid fcenes on fancy play ;
The lawn, of afpect fmooth and mild ;
The foreft-ground, grotefque and wild ;
The fhrub that fcents the mountain-gale ;
The ftream rough dafhing down the dale,
From rock to rock, in eddies toft ;
The diftant lake in which 'tis loft ;
Blue hills gay beaming thro' the glade ;
Lone urns that folemnize the fhade ;
Sweet interchange of all that charm
In groves, meads, dingles, rivulets, farms !
If aught the fair confufion pleafe,
Wifh lafting health, and lafting eafe,
To him who form'd the blifsful bower,
And gave thy life one tranquil hour ;
Wifh peace and freedom —thefe poffeft,
His temperate mind fecures the reft.

  But if thy foul fuch blifs defpife,
Avert thy dull incurious eyes ;
Go fix them there, where gems and gold,
Improv'd by art, their power unfold ;
Go try in courtly fcenes to trace
A fairer form of nature's face :
Go fcorn SIMPLICITY—but know,
That all our heart-felt joy's below,

                              That

That all which virtue loves to name,
Which art confligns to lafting fame,
Which fixes wit or beauty's throne,
Derives its fource from HER ALONE.

ARCADIO.

To WILLIAM SHENSTONE, *Efq; in his fickness*,

By *Mr* WOODHOUSE.

YE flow'ry plains, ye breezy woods,
    Ye bowers and gay alcoves,
Ye falling ftreams, ye filver floods,
    Ye grottoes, and ye groves!

Alas, my heart feels no delight,
    Tho' I your charms furvey;
While he confumes in pain the night,
    In languid fighs the day.

The flowers difclofe a thoufand blooms,
    A thoufand fcents diffufe;
Yet all in vain they fhed perfumes,
    In vain difplay their hues.

Reftrain, ye flowers, your thoughtlefs pride,
    Recline your gaudy heads;
And fadly drooping, fide by fide,
    Embrace your humid beds.

Tall oaks, that o'er the woodland fhade
    Your lofty fummits rear!
Ah why, in wonted charms array'd,
    Expand your leaves fo fair!

For lo, the flow'rs as gaily smile,
    As wanton waves the tree;
And tho' I sadly plain the while,
    Yet they regard not me.

Ah, should the fates an arrow send,
    And strike the fatal wound,
Who, who shall then your sweets defend,
    Or fence your beauties round?

But hark, perhaps the plumy throng
    Have learn'd my plaintive tale,
And some sad dirge, or mournful song,
    Comes floating in the gale.

Ah no! they chant a sprightly strain,
    To sooth an amorous mate;
Unmindful of my anxious pain,
    And his uncertain fate.

But see these little murmuring rills,
    With fond repinings rove;
And trickle wailing down the hills,
    Or weep along the grove.

Oh mock not if, beside your stream,
    You hear me too repine;
Or aid with sighs your mournful theme,
    And fondly call him mine.

Ye envious winds, the caufe difplay,
   In whifpers as ye blow,
Why did your treacherous gales convey
   The poifon'd fhafts of wo?

Did he not plant the fhady bower,
   Where you fo blithely meet?
The fcented fhrub, and fragrant flower,
   To make your breezes fweet?

And muft he leave the wood, the field,
   The dear Arcadian reign?
Can neither verfe nor virtue fhield
   The guardian of the plain?

Muft he his tuneful breath refign,
   Whom all the mufes love?
That round his brow their laurels twine,
   And all his fongs approve.

Preferve him, mild Omnipotence!
   Our Father, King, and God,
Who clear'ft the paths of life and fenfe,
   Or ftopp'ft them at thy nod.

Blefs'd pow'r, who calm'ft the raging deep,
   His valu'd health reftore,
Nor let the fons of Genius weep,
   Nor let the good deplore.

But

But if thy boundlefs wifdom knows
  His longer date an ill ;
Let not my foul a wifh difclofe
  To contradict thy will.

For happy, happy were the change,
  For fuch a god-like mind,
To go where kindred fpirits range,
  Nor leave a wifh behind.

And tho' to fhare his pleafures here,
  Kings might their ftate forego;
Yet muft he feel fuch raptures there,
  As none can tafte below.

VERSES left on a SEAT, *the hand unknown.*

O EARTH ! to his remains indulgent be,
 Who fo much care and coft beftow'd on thee !
Who crown'd thy barren hills with ufeful fhade,
And cheer'd with tinkling rills each filent glade;
Here taught the day to wear a thoughtful gloom,
And there enliven'd nature's vernal bloom.
Propitious earth ! lie lightly on his head,
And ever on his tomb thy vernal glories fpread !

        CORYDON.

CORYDON, A PASTORAL.

To the Memory of WILLIAM SHENSTONE, *Esq;*

I.

COME, shepherds, we'll follow the hearse,
　　And see our lov'd Corydon laid:
'Tho' sorrow may blemish the verse,
　　Yet let the sad tribute be paid.
They call'd him the pride of the plain:
　　In sooth he was gentle and kind;
He mark'd in his elegant strain,
　　The graces that glow'd in his mind.

II.

On purpose he planted yon trees,
　　That birds in the covert might dwell;
He cultur'd his thyme for the bees,
　　But never would rifle their cell.
Ye lambkins that play'd at his feet,
　　Go bleat—and your master bemoan:
His music was artless and sweet,
　　His manners as mild as your own.

III.

No verdure shall cover the vale,
　　No bloom on the blossoms appear;
The sweets of the forest shall fail,
　　And Winter discolour the year.
No birds in our hedges shall sing,
　　(Our hedges so vocal before),
Since he that should welcome the spring,
　　Can greet the gay season no more.

His

IV.

His Phillis was fond of his praife,
   And poets came round in a throng;
They liften'd, and envy'd his lays,
   But which of them equall'd his fong?
Ye fhepherds, henceforward be mute,
   For loft is the paftoral ftrain;
So give me my Corydon's flute,
   And thus—let me break it in twain.

J. CUNINGHAM.

F   I   N   I   S.